THE BOATBUILDER

THE
BOATBUILDER

DANIEL GUMBINER

McSWEENEY'S
SAN FRANCISCO

McSWEENEY'S
SAN FRANCISCO

McSweeney's and colophon are registered trademarks of McSweeney's, an independent publisher based in San Francisco. McSweeney's exists to champion ambitious and inspired new writing, and to challenge conventional expectations about where it's found, how it looks, and who participates. McSweeney's is a fiscally sponsored project of SOMArts, a nonprofit arts incubator in San Francisco.

Printed in the United States.

ISBN 978-1-944211-55-4

10 9 8 7 6 5 4 3 2 1

www.mcsweeneys.net

For my parents, Richard and Ellen Gumbiner

I have had an entirely new feeling about life ever since making an ax handle…

—E.B. White, in a letter to his wife

CHAPTER I

BERG CRACKED THE WINDOW and squeezed his way into the farmhouse. He had first seen this farmhouse while walking the dog on the hiking trail that circumnavigated the bay. In the morning the house seemed to be occupied, but during the day it was empty and often some of the windows were left open. People in Talinas always left their windows open. They were not used to thieves breaking and entering. Berg was not used to breaking and entering.

He went to the medicine cabinet first because that was the most likely place to find what he was looking for, but there was nothing of interest. Heart pills, vitamin supplements, deodorant, foot creams, and, strangely, Scotch tape. He moved back to the main room and began rifling through the drawers of a dresser. A seed catalogue, lots of photos of boats, two pairs of scissors, a dead black fly.

The next room appeared to be a study. There was an oilskin map and a large bookshelf and an old iMac, its case bright blue like some kind of tropical drink. Are you kidding me? he thought. The last time he had seen one of these computers was in elementary school, in the computer lab, and he had used it to play *Oregon Trail*. He had never been very good at *Oregon Trail*, too reckless with his decision-making. His oxen always died fording the river and the members of his party often ended up suffering from some kind of bowel-related disease.

It was a cold day, the day he entered the farmhouse, with a searching wind from the west and a layer of fog, low-slung and thick, covering the bay like marshmallow topping. But inside the house was warm and full of clear light. It smelled like cedar and coffee and salty air. If he hadn't been robbing the house, he would have liked to sit quietly in its living room and pass several hours reading a book. Whoever owned this place had a lot of beautiful furniture, including a dining table built from barn siding and a desk that seemed to have been carved out of the base of an oak tree.

Finding nothing useful in the living room, Berg made his way to the bedroom. A king-size bed and a window looking out on a grove of laurels and cedars. He thought he should be looking at the bay through this window but he couldn't see it. He felt a bit turned around. He was sweating now, a cold sweat that he felt primarily in his hands and feet. In the upper drawer of the bedroom closet he found what he was looking for: a bottle of

Lortab 7.5s. There was also a set of keys and a book of poems and some sort of amulet with an inscription in a foreign language. It seemed like the type of thing that would give him +2 dexterity.

Berg had spent the vast majority of seventh and eighth grade playing an online role-playing game called *Quest*. Every day, from the carpeted basement of his parents' suburban home, he battled orcs and traveled to foreign lands. His mother had to wrench him away from the computer to go to soccer practice or Hebrew school and, over time, she grew tired of this, and banned the game. She insisted that he read instead. Her father, Rabbi Joel Rothman, had been a genius Talmudic scholar and she often expressed, in overt and covert fashion, the hope that Berg would follow in his learned path.

"Such a sweet, wise man," she would say. And then always: "May he rest in peace."

Berg grabbed the Lortabs and went back to the main room, where he continued to open and close drawers. Suddenly, in the middle of his sifting, he felt compelled to go to the bathroom. Percocet made him constipated so these days he was often constipated. The constipation moved in bizarre cycles, an astrology he couldn't decipher. He would go days without being able to shit and then, all of a sudden, he'd have to shit very badly, which was what was happening to him right now, as he opened and closed drawers, looking for prescription medicine inside the farmhouse of a person he did not know.

He went to the bathroom because there was no other choice really. Well, there were other choices but they eluded him at the moment. It was a high-speed moment.

Things progressed well on the toilet but not as quickly as he'd hoped. In the middle of the process he heard a shuffle outside the door. He held still, which was not easy in that instant, and he listened closely. It was just house noises, he assured himself. When he was finished on the toilet he thought, for a second, about whether or not he should flush. If he flushed someone might hear him, but if he didn't there would be clear evidence of a break-in. He knew this was a thing that robbers did, break in and shit in the toilet and leave the shit there. Some kind of malevolent, scent-marking ritual.

He poured a glass of water and took four Lortabs. Then he flushed and left the house. Once outside, he found the trail on the ridge, and began walking home. The sun was setting now and the bay spread out before him, brown and ebbing, the color of pinto beans. Cows stood sedately in the fields and, every once in a while, a flock of cowbirds burst from the wet earth like black confetti. He could feel the Lortabs brimming inside him, warmth flooding his whole body, and soon, he knew, he would be in love with everything.

CHAPTER 2

BERG HAD MOVED TO Talinas a few weeks earlier to house-sit for Nell's friend's mom, who was traveling to Bali. Her name was Mimi. She was sixty-five and it was the first time she'd been out of the country. Mimi was retired and, in her retirement, she had devoted herself to pottery. She had many earth-toned coffee mugs and her yard was filled with ceramic bunnies, all of them standing stony watch like scouts in a frontier army. Mimi had left him a six-pack in the fridge and some eggs and several blocks of cheese. She also left him a long list of things to do, including watering the plants, caring for the chickens, and feeding and walking the dog, Fish. He was a leggy black dog who didn't like making eye contact. He was very smart but very anxious and whenever Berg reached out to pet him he would draw back and give him a skeptical, sideways glance. The chickens so far had proven easier to deal with. There were four of them and they were all named after state capitals: Sacramento, Atlanta, Baton Rouge, and Lansing.

Berg spent most nights at the Tavern. He would sit at the bar, stoned on Perc 30s, drinking beer and watching baseball games he didn't care about. He often ended up in conversations with the owner of the bar, a man named Ed Conotic, whose family also owned the other bar in town, the Western, which was located on the bay, next door to Vlasic's Boat Works. Ed Conotic hated Nick Vlasic and often told long, convoluted stories which concluded with Ed or one of Ed's family members suffering some grave miscarriage of justice at the hands of Nick Vlasic or one of Nick Vlasic's family members. Ed also liked to tell stories about his stepbrother, Gary Conotic, who, were it not for a freak staph infection caused by a dirty knee brace, might have made it in the NBA.

"He could shoot the lights out," Ed said. "Played on that team with Walt Weir that went to the state semifinals. Could shoot the lights out."

Ed was not really interested in listening to what Berg had to say, or what anyone had to say for that matter. He was one of these old men who seemed to have chosen his profession so that he would have a convenient and unassailable soap box from which he could express his opinions. This suited Berg fine: he was not very interested in discussing his life.

Also at the bar was Tom, an older rancher with coarse, unfinished features. Tom was slowly settling into dementia and he was no longer able to add sums well. Every time he settled up his tab, he'd count and recount his money, licking his finger before removing each dollar bill and placing it on the table.

"Oh hang on, let me start again," he'd say, shaking his head. Sometimes Ed Conotic came over and counted the money for him.

"You've got seven here, Tom. Three beers so you owe nine."

"Oh I knew I was missing a few. Knew I was missing a few."

There was John Coleman, too, the fisherman, and a younger guy he hung around with named Dennis Lapley. And there was Claire, an engineer for the water district, and her boyfriend, Lenny, and Joe Leggett, who delivered gas tanks and had fought in the Korean War and seemed to have a lot of hobbies. On Friday nights, there was a guy named Woody who played a thirty-minute set of his own country songs, which were mostly about deer.

"This song's about a deer I saw that went and disappeared behind a hillside," he would say. Or: "This is a song about two small deer and one medium deer that I saw on the road by the Dance Palace."

The only person Berg had talked to about pills was Lapley. Berg could tell he was an addict the moment he met him: the small bruises on his arms, the runny nose, the constant sniffing. Lapley was from Oregon but he'd worked in construction in Talinas for a few years now. Berg suspected that he was in his thirties but he wasn't sure. His eyes were small and dull and it seemed like the skin on his face had been stretched tight and then stapled across his jawline. Unlike Berg, Lapley shot up, and he once asked Berg if he wanted to join him in the bathroom.

"Nah, man," Berg said. "I stay away from needles."

"It's the same thing," Lapley said. "You're kidding yourself. It's the exact same thing."

Lapley said he was a volunteer with the Sheriff's Department and claimed he could arrest people. Berg didn't believe it. A dopehead volunteering with the Sheriff's Department? Lapley seemed to lie about almost every thing. But when he spoke about the two times he'd been through withdrawal, Berg had the sense that he was telling the truth. Lapley's descriptions reminded Berg of his own experience: sweats, muscle spasms, watery eyes, stomach cramps, violent shaking.

"I did it all on my own," Lapley boasted. "And I know, if I wanted to, I could do it again. Don't need no damn rehab center holding my hand."

Berg had gone to rehab. For the first two weeks they'd put him on Clonidine, Baclofen, Meloxicam, and Gabapentin; 50 mg Seroquel or 100 mg Trazodone to help him sleep. And then, after the first month, Clonidine as needed, Vistaril for anxiety, B_{12} vitamins, a slow tapering of his Gabapentin dose, peaking at 1600 mg. Antidepressants, too, mostly Wellbutrin, 150 mg, but also 30 mg of Prozac.

It was important to identify your triggers, they had told Berg, to know them and track them. Eliminate your supply. Remove the numbers from your phone. And he had done this, deleted Eugene's number from his phone, all the people he'd ever taken pills with. When the opportunity to house-sit for Mimi materialized, it seemed like a good first step toward reestablishing a sober life. If he moved up to Talinas, he could stay with Nell while also putting some tangible distance between himself and the world of his addiction.

But shortly after he moved up there he'd relapsed. He was over at Gloria and Jerry's for a neighborly dinner and, during a trip to the bathroom, he couldn't resist opening the medicine cabinet. Gloria and Jerry were old people and old people in America always had opioids. Like fifteen different kinds of opioids. It was as if they had been collecting them since the '60s, planning to bring them over to *Antiques Roadshow* and get them appraised.

The next couple of weeks were immensely pleasurable. Berg's stretch of abstinence had lowered his tolerance and he was able to get high in a way that had eluded him in the months prior to rehab. He stopped calling his sponsor, stopped going to the NA meetings in Pine Gulch. When his supply ran out, he began to casually enter homes that appeared unoccupied. He usually picked homes that were along the hiking trail, and he always carried a walking stick with him. If someone caught him, he would say he was lost and had been looking for some place to use a phone.

Every addict has a story about the impermanence of their addiction. For Berg, at this time, the return of Nell would constitute the end of his use. She was still on tour, had been on tour for the last two months. He was only doing this until she returned, having one last affair with opioids before he buckled down and endured sobriety for the rest of his life.

This was why he had gotten sober in the first place, why he had gone to rehab and quit his job at Cleanr and moved up here. He was sick of the city. It was all garbage and noise and men with gelled hair. He intended to go clean in more than one sense: he wanted to find work that was simple and fulfilling, to live a life of health and exercise and fresh air. But at the moment, these ambitions seemed distant.

One morning, after a night of drinking at the Tavern, he woke up with a headache. The headaches had a creepy, slinky quality at first, as if he were prey and they were stalking him. The pain was not there but he knew it was on its way, knew that a slight movement or sound could catalyze it. He took a couple of Vicodin and started a pot of coffee. While he was waiting for the coffee, he headed down to the coop to feed the chickens.

It took him a few moments to process the scene of carnage he encountered. One of the chickens, Baton Rouge, was missing and there were feathers and blood all over the plywood floor. Sacramento and Atlanta were pecking at Lansing, who appeared gravely wounded. Berg yelled at the two of them and shooed them away and then picked up Lansing, who had a bad wound near her neck. She shuddered in his arms and he whispered calming things in her ear. When she seemed still enough, he began walking toward the house.

He couldn't leave her outside but he couldn't let her run around loose inside Mimi's house either. In the end, he decided to place her inside Fish's crate. He pulled out Fish's bed, which was covered in black dog hair, and laid down newspaper for Lansing. Fish trotted over, clearly disturbed. He kept looking at the crate and then looking back at Berg, waiting for someone to explain this obvious injustice.

Back in the kitchen Berg consulted the note Mimi had left him and found the number he was looking for.

"If there are any problems with the animals," she had written, "call Ben at 415-327-6688."

Berg called Ben and began explaining, in great detail, what he had found in the chicken pen.

"Blood everywhere," he said, and then he repeated it: "everywhere!" As he relived the scene, the drama of the moment really took hold of him. He was a little stoned now, the headache receding but still there.

"I'll be right over," Ben said.

Ben was in his late thirties, with thinning hair and some kind of red streak in his right eye. He wore a white shirt with holes in it and a camouflage baseball hat. He had tattoos on his knuckles. Ben surveyed the coop for a minute and discovered a gap between two of the boards. He kneeled down, examined the crevice, and then issued his verdict:

"Looks like a coyote got 'em."

"A coyote?" Berg said.

"Yep, must have snuck right through here, picked his favorite chicken, and scurried off for a nice dinner."

Ben told Berg that he should build a wire fence around the coop. He said the fence should go down eighteen inches underground to prevent the coyotes from burrowing beneath it.

"And what do I do with the wounded chicken?"

"The wounded one? Where is she?"

"I put her in the dog crate."

Ben looked like he was about to say something but thought better of it.

"How bad is she injured?" he asked.

"Pretty badly," Berg said. "There's a big gash near her neck."

"From the coyote?"

"It seems like it. And the other chickens."

"Well, I would just put her out of her misery then," Ben said.

"Kill her?"

"Yeah, she's just going to suffer otherwise."

Berg thanked Ben for his help and walked back up to the house with a sick feeling in his stomach. This is what you have to do, he said to himself. You're helping the chicken. This is life in the country. This is nature. Coyotes attack chicken coops and chickens get weird neck wounds and then you have to kill them.

He walked into the kitchen and picked out the largest blade. It suddenly seemed like a very small blade and he wondered whether Mimi had something larger he could use. He looked through the shed but the only potential substitute he found was a pair of garden shears, but this seemed cruel, medieval somehow.

Back in the kitchen, he opened the liquor cabinet and grabbed a bottle of whiskey. He took a long pull, winced, and then picked up the knife. When he turned around he noticed that Fish was several feet away, staring at him. *What will this guy do next?* he seemed to be saying. *He is out of his mind.* Berg gripped the knife tightly and walked over to the dog crate. He knelt by the crate and began cooing to the chicken as if she were a cat. Berg had only ever owned cats and all the noises he made toward animals were cat noises.

"Come on out, Lansing," he said. "Come on, sweet girl."

But the chicken did not want to come out. She had been attacked by a coyote and then attacked by her fellow chickens, whom, Berg imagined, she'd probably considered her friends, and now she was finally safe in this strange plastic box and there was no way she was going to come out. She scurried to the back of the crate where Berg could not reach her. It was a big crate. Fish was a big dog.

"Come on now," Berg said, reaching for her with one hand and holding the knife with the other. "Come on out here."

He thought about trying to kill the chicken while it was still inside the crate but this seemed difficult, physics-wise, and then there would be blood all over the crate and Fish would never forgive him. He set the knife down on the kitchen table and paced around the room thinking about what he should do. He could call Ben again and ask him for help. He could try tipping the crate upside down. Or he could let the chicken live. This option began to take hold of him. He had never wanted to kill the chicken in the first place, he thought. That was Ben's idea. Why not let her live inside the crate?

He walked out to the coop and filled a bowl with chicken feed. The other two chickens were sitting silently on their straw, as though nothing important had happened that morning. "You've shown your true colors," Berg said aloud to the chickens. "Pecking an injured friend. Kicking her when she was down. You guys are sick."

Back at the house he placed the bowl of chicken feed in the dog crate along with a teacup of water. Then he read online about how to care for a wounded chicken. They recommended putting the chicken in a dark place with some kind of heating lamp, so he brought over an electric heater and he draped a blanket on top of the crate. Fish stood by the whole time, the permanence of the situation beginning to dawn on him.

When the crate was fixed up, Berg made himself a bowl of cereal, sat down at the kitchen table, and e-mailed Mimi to tell her what had happened. After he wrote the e-mail he began to look through his inbox. A newsletter from the hippie temple in the city he'd gone to once or twice for the High Holidays. A link to a basketball highlight from his brother. And, finally, an e-mail from Nell: the band was back in California now and she'd be home in a week.

He walked back over to the crate and looked at Lansing. Blood all over her feathers but no blood dripping. Outside, a light rain was falling. Morning calls of birds and the bark of a dog and, in the distance, the grind and rip of a circular saw. He picked up the teacup of water and held it to the chicken.

"Drink," he said. "You need to drink."

CHAPTER 3

THE MORNING AFTER THE chicken attack Berg looked through job postings online. He was going to do what he'd come here to do in the first place. He'd find a permanent place to live in Talinas and he'd get a job. He'd do a seven-day taper and get clean by the time Nell returned. He didn't need the Clonidine and the Gabapentin. He'd only relapsed for a few weeks and his withdrawal wouldn't be that bad.

"A successful taper is like walking a razor's edge," he read online. "You're trying to keep these two opposing forces at bay: the withdrawal and the addiction."

But he'd do it. He had plenty of pills to taper with and he'd handle it himself and not have to return to rehab. By the time Nell got home he'd be fine and it would be as if this whole binge had never happened.

There were not many jobs listed in Talinas. An ad for a sous chef, a concierge at an inn, a registered dental assistant. The most intriguing posting said: "Sailboat Maintenance Worker: NO PREVIOUS EXPERIENCE NECESSARY."

Berg had never been on a sailboat in his life. He'd always found the world of boats romantic, but intimidating. It seemed like the type of thing you only did if you'd grown up in some heavily ivied town in Connecticut. He called the number. A tired-sounding man picked up.

"Yes?"

"Hi, my name is Berg and I'm interested in the boat maintenance job."

"The what?"

"The boat maintenance job?"

"Oh, that. You want to talk to Garrett."

"Garrett?"

"Yeah, just come in later today."

"What time?"

"I dunno. Can you come in now?"

"Sure," Berg said.

"Yeah, just come in now then."

Berg drove along the eastern edge of the bay. It was a long narrow bay and it lay directly on a fault line: the meeting of the North American plate and the Pacific plate. The western side of the bay was dry and smelled like granite and dust and pine. The eastern side was more swampy and smelled like swamp. The town was located at the northeast corner of the bay. It had a feed barn and a café and a bar and several gift shops that sold new-agey wares: mermaid art and Tibetan bowls and palo santo. There was also a library, a bakery, a tractor rental store, and a few restaurants. Berg figured he could probably get a job at the Tavern if all else failed, but hanging around that bar didn't seem like the best idea. He wanted to do something physical, something that required an able body every morning.

When he reached the south end of the bay, he took a right and turned up a freshly paved drive. FERNWOOD, a sign said, A PEERLESS CLUB. He parked and walked up to the clubhouse, resume in hand. A family of five rushed past him, laughing and smiling, their hair shiny and blond. They were all wearing collared shirts, except for the mother, who was wearing fluorescent running clothes.

The clubhouse smelled like fresh laundry and sweat and chlorine. There was no one at the front desk so Berg rang the bell. While he waited, he picked up a pamphlet on the desk in front of him and began to read. "Being a Fernwood Member sure has its perks," it said. "Find out about the valuable services and benefits available to all Fernwood Members—just because you're you."

"Can I help you?" Berg looked up and greeted the woman who had appeared behind the desk. She was wearing a white collared shirt and her face was freckled like a tortilla. He told her he was looking for Garrett.

"I think he's down by the water," the woman said.

"Which way is the water?"

She pointed behind herself, at a painting of a fern.

"Here's his cell phone number in case you can't find him." She wrote the number down on a pink Post-it and handed it to Berg.

Down at the dock he looked around for Garrett. He tried calling the cell phone number but it went straight to voicemail ("It's Garrett," the message said). There were probably twenty boats along the pier and several more hauled out on land. The bay was calm, the morning windless and warm. A man emerged from the galley of one of the boats. He was holding a spray bottle in one hand and a cigarette in the other. He puffed the cigarette and spat off the edge of the boat, brown tobacco spit. Then he turned around and yelled at someone in the galley. A short, chubby man emerged. He was wearing a hemp necklace and cargo pants.

"I looked at the October 15 thing," the shorter man said. "That thing looks fucking awesome. They're opening up the show. Oh, what's it called? Shit, I already forgot it. It's um… a classic motorcycle thing on the grass."

"Oh, it's part of that," the cigarette man said.

"It's really cool."

"It's ridiculously cool."

"I don't think I'm gonna ride the bike there, though."

"Why not? It's an easy ride."

"I don't know how much power it puts out," the shorter man said.

"Just ride the 1. Don't take the 5. Go super fucking early and take the damn 1."

"Plus I haven't found a cheap used regulator box yet."

"Just get a new regulator box, Simon. Go to Grainger."

"Grainger? They have motorcycle parts?"

"That's not a motorcycle part, Simon."

"Isn't it a Bosch part?"

"Bosch is not motorcycles."

"It's not?"

"Bosch is one of the largest…" the cigarette man trailed off, sighed, and then continued. "Bosch is one of the largest electronics manufacturers in the world. None of that electronic stuff is motorcycles, Simon. I told you that."

By this time Berg had walked down to the boat where the two men were standing.

"Garrett?" Berg interjected, looking at the cigarette man.

"Oh shit," the man said. "Hey. You must be the uh... the guy." He punched out his cigarette on the heel of his shoe and stuck the butt in his pocket. It was a Black & Mild and the smell reminded Berg of childhood, of smoking blunts behind the bleachers at his high school. Berg shook Garrett's hand and then handed him a resume.

"Brought this for you," he said. Garrett began to look over his resume and Simon nodded at Berg.

"How's it going?" Simon said.

"All right," Berg replied. After a few seconds Garrett handed the resume back to Berg and lit another Black & Mild.

"You're totally qualified," he said. "Totally qualified."

"I've never worked on boats before."

"You're definitely qualified."

"Are you sure?"

"Yeah man. I'm giving you a job. What's your deal?"

"Okay."

"You'll go out on your first charter tomorrow."

"What do you mean charter?"

"We charter a Gulfstar 50 on the bay. Name's S/V *Blown Away*. You'll be crew. Did it not say that in the ad?"

"No, it just said maintenance."

"Fucking Mangini. I told him to list it as maintenance and charter crew, did I not, Simon?"

"You did," Simon said. "As I recall you did."

"Well, we're gonna teach you everything anyway," Garrett said.

"I have no sailing experience," Berg said.

"Like I said, we're going to teach you. Well, Simon's going to teach you. For now, though, I want you to clean the galleys on all of these boats with Simon."

He handed Berg the spray bottle.

"There are rags in the dock box," Garrett said. Then he hopped off the boat and began walking up the hill, toward the clubhouse.

"Come find me when you're done," he called over his shoulder.

CHAPTER 4

THE YACHT CLUB HAD an extensive fleet of dinghies and keel-boats. Lessons were open to members and non-members but they were mostly attended by members. Once members attained certain qualifications, they were able to reserve boats and sail them without instructors. Most days, Berg, Garrett, and Simon performed maintenance on the yacht club's fleet, but they also crewed on the club's charter boat. According to Garrett, several years ago Mangini had convinced the owner of the yacht club, Lucas Vespucci, to dip his toe into the world of chartering. He said there were several companies already doing it on the bay, mostly based out of Five Brooks, and they were making a killing. Vespucci bought a Gulfstar 50 for a hundred thousand dollars and sank a hundred thousand more into it to get the boat to pass Coast Guard inspection. For the past four years she had sailed as a charter boat but she had not come close to recovering Vespucci's initial investment. Apparently, Mangini was under pressure to book more charters this season or risked getting fired. As a result, Garrett was under pressure to book charters, and he resented this a great deal.

"I can't control who books and who doesn't book," he said. "He wants me chartering and he wants me doing all the maintenance and he wants me fixing Vespucci's dad's canoe. I don't know, man. I can't be in a thousand places at once."

"Maybe if you spent less time smoking in the parking lot we'd get the maintenance done more quickly," Simon said.

"Simon, say that one more time and see what I do."

"Stop smoking in the parking lot."

"One more time."

"Stop smoking in the parking lot."

"One more time."

"I already said it twice."

"That's what I thought, bro," Garrett said. "Step down."

S/V *Blown Away* was a large, clumsy vessel designed for retired couples who wanted to go cruising in Mexico. The boat was almost always captained by Garrett but, on occasion, Mangini hired an old British man named Carl to captain her. There were also several other part-time crew, including a young woman named Shawnecee. She wore skate shoes and jeans and she had just come back from French Polynesia, where she'd been sailing on an educational tall ship. She said she was in Talinas for the summer to make some cash and then she was heading to

Alaska. The first day Berg worked with her, he went down into the galley and saw a note on the whiteboard that said, "I love you Shawnecee. You're doing a great job. —Garrett"

When he went abovedecks again, he found Shawnecee counting out life vests. Garrett always liked to have them ready before the charter began.

"Me and Garrett got in a fight this morning," she said.

"About what?" Berg asked.

"There were potato chips all over the deck from the charter yesterday. I meant to hose them down before he arrived but my bike had a flat and he beat me to the docks."

"Well, he seems to have forgiven you."

"What do you mean?"

"The note below. On the whiteboard."

"Oh no, I wrote that," Shawnecee said. "He's gonna be so pissed when he sees it. Doesn't matter though. He can't say shit to me. We started working for Mangini at the same time. I know just as much as he does."

The boat was usually chartered by tourists or corporations that wanted to do some kind of adventure outing for their employees. On rare occasions, the boat was booked by locals to celebrate a birthday and, once, the boat had been booked for a Greek wedding.

"They had all these rituals," Garrett said. "They poured a jar of black sand into a jar of normal sand. It was meant to symbolize... what was it meant to symbolize, Simon?"

"It was basically just like a bar mitzvah," Simon said.

"It was not a bar mitzvah, Simon. It was a wedding."

"It reminded me of a bar mitzvah."

In general, they picked up passengers at Pier 4, near Talinas, and sailed them around the bay for two hours, usually during sunset. Garrett and Simon did most of the sailing and Berg, as second mate, served food and drinks. Garrett bought all of the food at a discount grocery store: hummus variety packs, sliced cheeses, potato chips, and, if the client had ordered the "deluxe food package," deli sandwiches. Mangini didn't want the clients to know where the food came from so Berg was required to take it out of its packaging in the galley and serve it on a platter or in a white bowl. Whenever anyone asked where the food came from, Garrett said they had a "private caterer."

If there was down time during a charter, Simon would show Berg how to do certain things on the boat. He learned how to raise the mainsail and how to use a winch handle and how to tie a bowline. The work wasn't exhausting but it was physical. He liked how his body was pleasantly fatigued at the end of the day, how his skin smelled like sun.

Berg was down to about four pills a day, but he was having a hard time reducing his dose further. He was, he knew, terrified of withdrawal, traumatized by his first experience of it. His whole body wracked with pain, bone-deep pain, and freezing cold. Always the cold in the morning, icy and dry, as if he'd slept in the frozen food aisle of the supermarket. Yawning and sneezing. Diarrhea and sticky chemical sweat. His body expelling fluid through every orifice available, it seemed, except for his ears.

Now that he had a job he had begun to look at places to move, but it was difficult to find affordable housing in Talinas. He talked to one guy who wanted to rent out his trailer and an older woman who wanted a live-in caretaker. He looked for housing in Five Brooks, Glen Meadow, and Palomarin, but he couldn't find any-thing. Palomarin was closer to the eastern suburban corridor and much more expensive, and Glen Meadow and Five Brooks were so small that there were never any places for rent.

Lansing's health was steadily improving, and every morning Berg inspected her closely, resupplied her with food and water. He thought she needed to be moved out of the crate, to a larger enclosure, but he was reticent to return her to the coop. She still appeared weak and he feared that the other chickens would attack her. He decided to build her a small coop out of redwood siding and two-by-fours that he found behind the house. He was getting better with his hands now: he had picked up a few tips from Garrett and Simon and he trusted himself with the contours of basic construction.

He spent too much time building the coop, outfitting it with several embellishments, including a circular door and windowsill flowers. When he was finished, he brought Lansing out to her new home. As he watched her flap around inside the coop, he was filled with a sense of accomplishment. It was all out of proportion with what he had done, but it was a nice feeling.

CHAPTER 5

NELL HAD BROWN HAIR and green eyes and a dimple in her nose the size of a pea. She worked in film as a freelance wardrobe assistant but she wanted to make her living as a musician. For the past couple of months she'd been opening for a band named Carlos Carlos de Carlos, who had heard her play at a house show in the city and invited her on their tour. It was the longest tour she'd ever done, from San Francisco to Atlanta, but it was finally over and she was back at her place in the city and coming up to see him in Talinas.

The day she visited, they hiked the trail that ran along Sausal Creek and down to Miller's Point. It was a warm day, with no fog, and all along the trail there were orange monkey flowers and sweet-smelling sagebrush. Berg brought sandwiches, a thermos of coffee, and a couple of bananas. As they walked toward the point, they passed a group of young men who were fishing. Nell greeted them and asked them what they had caught.

"Rays, mostly," one of the men said.

"What are you trying to catch?" Nell asked.

The man thought for a moment. "I guess… whatever," he said.

"Whatever," Nell repeated.

"Yeah, whatever," he said, shrugging.

They walked past the men, out to the point, and sat down on the grass with a crunch. Berg looked out at the water, which was full of small pale waves. Nell inspected her arm.

"I think I might have brushed some poison oak back there," she said.

Nell was extremely allergic to poison oak. She seemed to get it every other time she went on a hike. When she was a junior in high school, she got it all around her mouth because she'd rubbed her face with a mango skin, which, it turns out, has the same toxin as poison oak. She toured colleges like this, the allergic skin red and swollen, ringing her lips like a goatee. Berg had seen photos.

"Seems okay to me," Berg said, looking at the arm in question.

"It can take days to show up," Nell said. "It's okay. I'll just wash myself with the poison oak soap when I get home. I brought some."

Berg handed Nell her sandwich. She took a bite and looked back toward the fishermen.

"People fish over there a lot," Berg said, following her gaze.

"I get it," Nell said. "It seems like a great place to hang out. Bring a few beers, sit in the sun, catch some whatever fish."

Berg laughed. "Lean this way," he said. "I want to take a picture of you. The light is so good."

"With or without sandwich?"

"With."

He took out his phone and aimed the camera. Nell pursed her lips, opened her eyes wide like she'd just heard something very surprising.

"Relax," he said. "You always make a weird face."

"I can't help it."

She tried to strike a different pose but only looked stiffer, more self-conscious.

"Don't be weird," Berg said. "Just be yourself."

"I'm weird in photos," Nell replied. "That is myself."

After their picnic, Berg drove Nell over to Talinas and showed her around town. They bought a fancy cheese and stopped at the bakery for a cinnamon bun. They were heading to the car when Berg saw Lapley. He was standing on the other side of Main Street, next to the Station House diner, and leafing through the local paper. Nell would know what that friendship was about right away. Berg lowered his baseball cap over his eyes and picked up the pace. They were in the car and on the road before Lapley looked up from the news. Berg took a deep breath and put on a new podcast he'd been listening to.

"Have you heard this show?" he said to Nell. "I think you'll like it."

That night they cooked sausages and drank beer. When Berg drank he always wanted opioids and, at one point, he snuck off to his secret stash in the bedroom. He swallowed three Lortabs and then immediately felt a wave of shame. He'd come so far over the past couple of weeks but here he was, taking three pills at a time. If Nell knew, she'd be so disappointed. She smoked and drank but she'd never had a problem with substances. She always knew how far to push that kind of thing. It seemed intuitive for her. Nell had good intuition when it came to many things. Her best friend Jo often said that she'd "been born knowing how to live."

They went to bed early, slipping into boxers and T-shirts. Nell lay on her back and smoked a joint while he kissed her neck. People always described opioid users as taking pills and then collapsing into the couch, their tongues lolling out the side of their mouths. But that's not how it felt at all. Berg's whole body surged with an overwhelming sense of well-being and energy. He was able to feel his feelings in a pure, unmediated fashion, like he could when he was a child.

Nell put out the joint and rolled onto his chest. Boxers off, underwear off, slow at first, Nell on top, Berg's feet and hands sweaty, Nell's T-shirt still on, billowing before her like a kite. Then fast and hot, Mimi's platform bed squeaking, Nell's shirt off, Berg on top, his face buried in her hair, that Nell hair smell, ocean and honey and mint. An untraceable passage of time, perhaps elongated or compressed, who could say, certainly distorted, warped, sweaty and breathy and then, Nell coming, gulping in air, squeezing his arms, gasping. He finished with his head buried in the pillow, his heart beating *thud thud thud*, his chest uncorked.

Nell grabbed the towel next to the bed, arched her back up, and placed the towel beneath her. He slid out and she folded the towel over, wiped herself clean. She threw the towel onto the floor and rolled over onto a pillow. Berg looked out the window. A moth torpedoed into the glass, staggered backward upon impact, and then torpedoed once again.

"These are your sheets, aren't they?" Nell said. "If we ever move in together we're not using these flannel sheets."

"Why not?"

"Because you always sweat so much in them."

"I sweat in all sheets," Berg said. "It's just one my things. I sweat at night. I think it's an Ashkenazi Jew thing. I know a lot of Ashkenazis who sweat at night."

"Okay," Nell said. "All I'm saying is you sweat more in the flannel."

Berg disagreed but didn't want to pursue the argument. "Maybe," he offered. "Do you want any water?"

"Sure."

He stood up and walked to the bathroom sink, filled two glasses. This took a long time. Mimi's bathroom sink had terrible water pressure. The flow was so weak that it could not clear hairs from his razor when he shaved. He had to use the bathtub faucet instead, which was a cumbersome process, and made him shave less than usual. As he filled the glasses, he thought about how nice it was to see Nell, how much he wanted her to stay. If you had asked him a few weeks ago if he was lonely in Talinas, he would have said no. But now that Nell was here, he didn't want her to go.

"It's so quiet here," Nell said as he handed her a glass. "I'm going to sleep so well."

"I think you'd really like it up here," Berg said.

"I do like it up here."

"No, I mean, if you moved up here, with me. I think you'd like it."

Nell sat up straight, brushed her hair out of her eyes.

"We talked about that before you moved," she said. "I need to be in the city right now. This was our plan. I love coming up here to visit."

"This is the first time you've come up."

"And I'm *loving it*. I just got back. What do you want me to say?"

"I know it's not what we planned," Berg said, "but I guess it's just… it's lonelier up here than I anticipated."

"So you're saying it's good to see me," Nell said.

Berg grinned. He wasn't sure what he was saying.

"You need to get out and meet some people," she said, encouragingly. "I was talking about this with Jo the other day: how so many men I know seem to grow more isolated as they get older. My uncle, for example. I'm not saying you're growing isolated. I'm just saying it seems like a challenge for men as they age, to keep friendships alive."

Berg felt immediately defensive. Was she saying he was a loner? He was not a loner. He had lots of friends from college, and he'd had friends in the city. But when was the last time he called any of them or saw them? The only people he hung out with these days were Garrett and Simon and they were not exactly his friends. He thought about all the time he'd spent by himself the past couple of weeks, building Lansing's coop. He was closing in on himself, Nell was right. Even when he lived in the city he hadn't really had any close friends. A few coworkers he would get drinks with and a couple of guys, like Eugene, whom he partied with. Most of the time he hung out with Nell's friends. They were his friends, too, but in a secondary way. He certainly hadn't seen any of them since he moved to Talinas.

"Relax your brow," Nell said, stroking his forehead with the back of her hand. "Your brow is all scrunched up."

Berg tried to relax the muscles in his face, blinked a few times. Nell moved in to kiss him. It was a good, long kiss. When it was over she leaned back against the headboard, stared down at her shins.

"Man," she said, "I really need to shave my leg hair."

CHAPTER 6

FRIDAY MORNING, BERG BIKING along the 1, his feet sore, his back sore, the specter of a headache on the horizon. The 1 ran north to south along the bay, and from there forked inland for a bit until it nosed its way out to Jensen Beach. After that it continued south, disappearing into the city, only to emerge, miles later, along the cliffs of Pacifica. Cyclists often cruised the 1, wending their way up to Talinas, where they stopped to buy coffee and pastries and admire the feed barn. On the weekend, they swarmed the town, and you would see them meandering from shop to shop, walking in the funny way the cyclists walked, on their heels, like penguins.

Berg had gotten a headache around the same time yesterday, as he was biking to work. It had lasted the whole day and into the night. The headaches made sleep difficult and, this morning, he had woken up feeling unrooted, foggy, as if he'd been drinking whiskey the night before. He reached for the glass of water next to the bed, took a sip, and then spit out the water. It tasted terrible, like a dirty puddle. He'd forgotten that he'd left the glass there for the past three days. He got up and threw the rest of the water into the potted fern by the bed, walked to the kitchen. The sun was already up so he made coffee and toast. While he waited for the coffee to brew, he washed a few dishes in the sink, lathering them in lemony soap.

He thought about calling in sick, but he'd already done that a couple of times earlier in the month, when he'd taken too many Lortabs and slept through his alarm. After Nell's visit, he'd started taking more pills again. It wasn't until he missed multiple days of work that he realized his tapering project had failed. He decided he would quit cold turkey instead.

The next two weeks, without any opioids at all, were excruciating. Constant headaches, his whole body in a state of general discomfort. He took a lot of acetaminophen and ibuprofen but it wasn't the same. He had very little energy and he suffered from diarrhea and nausea. At work he was always sneaking off to the staff outhouse by the water or running to the head if they were on a charter. One day Garrett saw him leaving the outhouse for the third time that morning and he gave him a pitying look.

"Whatever Chinese restaurant you're going to," Garrett said, "I would stop going to it. That's my advice to you."

So here he was today, another headache looming, biking toward Fernwood. They were scheduled to do a charter out of Pier 4 at 11:00. It was BYO, which meant that Berg would have to serve whatever kind of food and drinks the clients brought. BYOs could work in your favor or they could be terrible. Sometimes people brought almost no food and drink and Berg was able to help Simon sail the whole trip. Other times people brought twelve bottles of rose and got drunk and Berg had to clean vomit out of the head. One time, a woman brought an elaborate fondue setup and Berg found himself heating cheese in a cauldron on the cabin top.

Berg and Simon refueled the boats in the marina and then began prepping *Blown Away* for the charter. They put the deck gear on deck, tested the engine, clipped in the halyard, secured all the hatches. By 10 a.m. they had cast off and were en route to Pier 4. Simon was steering the boat and Berg and Garrett were sitting below the dodger. Garrett seemed to be in a particularly buoyant mood.

"Going to the Oysters game later tonight," he said.

The Muire County Oysters were the local minor-league baseball team. Their mascot was a talking oyster that looked more like a frog than an oyster. People around the county had signs in front of their homes that said SHUCK 'EM UP. GO OYSTERS.

"Who's pitching?" Simon asked.

"Santorini," Garrett said.

"Oh yeah, Santorini. He's good."

"He's really good. He's probably the best Oysters pitcher of all time. If not the best, then at least in the top three."

"What about Lew Brown?" Simon said.

"He's in the top three, too."

"Who else is in the top three?"

"There's one other. That's why it's a top three."

"Who is it?"

"I'm not going to feed everything to you like a baby bird, Simon. Go get a history book. Educate yourself."

"You're not going to tell me 'cause you don't know."

"What?"

"You just made up this arbitrary list."

"Is the galley clean, Simon? Berg, come steer for a bit. You need the practice and Simon needs to clean the galley.

When they got close to Pier 4, Garrett took the wheel and Berg kicked over the fenders, draped the dock lines along the lifelines for easy access. Garrett brought the boat in at an angle and then threw it into reverse, using the prop walk to swing the stern around. After Berg had made fast the dock lines, he came back on board and began placing life vests on deck.

"How many people are we?" he asked Garrett.

"Twelve. So fifteen life vests. Make sure you text Mangini after we're underway, too."

Once Berg set up the life vests, he gathered the liability waivers and stepped off the boat onto the pier. Garrett was sitting on top of a dock box, talking to the client on his cell phone.

"What did you say? You're at Pier 1½? Why are you at Pier 1½? Yeah, we had you scheduled for 12:00 at Pier 4. Two-hour cruise. You guys said you were bringing an ice cream cake. Right. There's a boat there already? You must have double-booked. Yeah. I don't know how. We don't pick up at Pier 1½. What's the Captain's name? Billy? Yeah, okay, and how many people are you again? Twelve. Perfect. Thanks, Todd. Well, you head off with them. We'll settle this up tomorrow over the phone. Okay. Enjoy yourself. Yeah, no problem. No, no, really it's no problem."

He hung up and pumped his fist.

"Yes, yes, yes!" he shouted. "We are going to nail those fuckers. I am going to nail Billy. He's been doing this for years."

"Doing what?" Berg asked.

"Chartering out of Pier 1½ with a six-pack license. He is not licensed to carry twelve passengers. Do you know how much it cost us to get *Blown Away* to pass Coast Guard inspection? And these guys are fucking stealing charters out from under our noses with insufficient licenses. But oh, we're gonna destroy 'em. We're gonna destroy 'em. I am so pumped."

He climbed down into the galley and called the Coast Guard. A young man picked up and Garrett put him on loudspeaker. Garrett always put calls on loudspeaker.

"United States Coast Guard Sector Eleven," the man said.

"Good afternoon. I want to report an illegal charter that is happening right now, departing from Pier 1½." Garrett was rubbing his jaw, pacing back and forth in the small galley.

"Okay, sir, what can you tell me about the charter?"

"It is motor vessel *Chico Rico*, that's M/V *Chico Rico*, and it's departing from Pier 1½ as we speak with twelve passengers and the captain is only licensed with a six-pack, and I know this because they were supposed to be my charter but they were taken out from under my nose."

"Sir, we currently have a rescue taking place along the coast. We will probably have to handle this administratively. Or we'll board the vessel next time we see it. In any case, we'll have an investigator give you a call tomorrow."

"But they're gonna deny it," Garrett said. "There will be no evidence."

"I'm sorry sir, but we don't have the capacity to address the issue at this time."

The Coast Guard officer hung up.

"Motherfuckers," Garrett said. "We'll go it alone."

"What?" Berg said.

"You heard me. We'll go it alone."

"What does that mean?"

"I'm not scared of anyone, man. I'm not scared of anyone. Cast off the dock lines, Berg."

"Oh yeah," Simon said. "We're gonna get these fuckers."

They motored over to Pier 1½ but by the time they got there *Chico Rico* had departed. There was nothing around except an abandoned orange motorboat with a broken windshield and a seagull pecking at fish guts. Berg's headache was steadily emerging. He did not want to chase down M/V *Chico Rico* so they could narc them out to the Coast Guard, but Garrett and Simon were galvanized, and Berg sensed that the trip was far from over.

"They probably went to Horse Island," Simon said. "Probably doing a little spin around Horse Island."

"Good idea," Garrett said.

They motored southwest toward the island. Simon steered and Garrett scanned the bay with his binoculars. Berg went to the bow, held onto the forestay, and surveyed the bay. There were a few other boats out but no sign of *Chico Rico*. A platoon of cormorants flew low along the shore and Muire birds dipped their heads in and out of the cold water. The shiny back of a seal appeared and then slipped below the surface. At the bow, Simon and Garrett could not see him, and Berg was able to close his eyes. This held the headache at bay to a certain extent. He was able to keep his eyes closed for several minutes, until Simon shouted.

"Over there!" he said. "It's them."

Chico Rico was a thirty-five-foot motorboat with a small galley. There were grooves running along her hull to present the illusion of wooden planking but she was made out of fiberglass. The boat was heading straight at them, slightly to port. Simon throttled down as the vessels neared each other.

"Get your phone ready," Garrett shouted at Berg. "We're going to take photos when we pass them."

A few minutes later the boats passed each other, port to port, and Garrett and Berg casually took photos. Berg tried to act like he was checking something on his phone and not photographing the other boat. It was hard to say if there were twelve people on board but there were certainly more than six. Once they passed the boat, Berg looked back at its stern: there were two men sitting in wooden chairs, drinking white wine from stemless glasses. Berg waved at them and they waved back.

"Beautiful day," one of them called.

"It is a beautiful day," Garrett answered. "It is so beautiful."

CHAPTER 7

TO BERG'S SURPRISE, THE Coast Guard followed through on its word and boarded *Chico Rico* the following day. Billy called Garrett from the water.

"Did you sic the Coast Guard on me?" Billy said. Garrett was down by the docks with Simon and Berg, refitting a window on one of the Santanas.

"I may have," Garrett said. "Look, it's been a long week. Hard to remember what I did or did not do."

"I have six Coasties up my ass right now and I know it was your doing."

"Please don't use that foul language, Billy. Simon is right next to me and he is an impressionable young man."

"This isn't over, Garrett."

"Don't get mad, Billy."

"Oh, I'm mad."

Billy, Berg learned, was the brother of Deputy White, one of the two sheriffs in town. They both grew up in Five Brooks but now they lived in Talinas. Billy was unmarried and had worked for the county water district as a groundwater consultant. According to Simon he had a "light meth problem." Garrett was concerned that Billy's brother was going to find a way to bail him out so he called the Sheriff's Department after he hung up with Billy to lodge a formal complaint.

"I want it on the record that there may be a conflict of interest within the Sheriff's Department, stemming from a major maritime fine issued to the brother of a deputy," Garrett said.

"My brother got a big fine?" Deputy White said.

"He was violating Coast Guard rules. Look, I don't want to see anyone go down, but the playing field's got to be level. This unlevel playing field is good for no one."

"What did he get fined for?"

"Had too many passengers on a charter."

"So someone tipped off the Coast Guard that he had too many people on board?"

"Evidently."

"Okay, Garrett, it's on the record."

"Thank you, Deputy White."

CHAPTER 8

ONE SATURDAY, BERG DROVE down to the city to give Nell a surprise visit. It had been weeks since he'd left Talinas and he wanted to get out of town. As he drove along the 1, he passed ferns and cypresses and pines, columns of weathered roadside rock. Out on the water he could see the combers rolling in, foamy and slow, exhausted after their cross-ocean journey and eager to break upon the shore.

For the people of Talinas, leaving the bay was a big deal. They referred to anything beyond the town as "over the hill," and traveling over the hill was generally regarded as undesirable and troublesome. "You'll have to go over the hill to get that" was something people usually said in a resigned, sorrowful tone. Some people seemed to never go over the hill. According to Garrett, there was a local artist who had not left the town once in the last twenty years.

Berg drove past Glen Meadow and Alamere and Jensen Beach, with its corner deli and its empty basketball court, everything salty and still and cool. From there, he headed inland toward the eastern suburban corridor, where the highway was lined with big-box stores and fast-food chains, and eventually he made his way across the bridge and out toward the sandswept western half of the city. There was no traffic the whole way and he arrived at Nell's apartment in two hours.

"Berg! What the hell?" Nell said. "Come in. I was just going to make coffee. Actually, let's go out for coffee. Want to go out?"

"Sure, yeah, I'm easy."

They walked to the coffee shop around the corner. It only sold coffee, toast, and coconut water, and it always had a line. Today, the line was particularly long. It stretched back to the far wall, which featured someone's collage art. Berg and Nell had been standing in the line for a few moments when he saw Kenneth, his old coworker, by the counter. He'd just ordered his coffee and he was about to turn around, at which point Berg would be right in his line of sight. Berg wished the collage-art wall were some kind of permeable membrane, that he could just slip through it and disappear into the street. But there he was and there was Kenneth.

"What's up, Berg?" he said. He was wearing a V-neck and running shorts and he looked like he was about to go play softball in the park with old college friends.

"Hi Kenneth," Berg said. "Do you remember my girlfriend, Nell?"

"Hi," Nell said.

"Oh, hi," Kenneth said, and then he looked back at Berg. "I haven't seen you in forever. What are you doing?"

"I'm up in Talinas," Berg said

"Is that like in Oregon?" Kenneth asked.

"No, it's just a couple hours north."

"Oh, right on. Cool, cool. Well, you know we miss you at the office. I know we never worked together directly, but everyone told me you were killing it."

"Thanks, yeah…"

"So what're you doing up there in… uh…"

"Talinas."

"Yeah, what're you doing up there?"

"I'm working a boat maintenance job."

"Really?" Kenneth said. It seemed like he thought Berg was playing a joke on him.

"And you're sailing," Nell added.

"That too," Berg said. "I help take people out on sailing charters."

"Like, you sail the actual boat?" Kenneth asked.

"Yes."

"Whoa, dude. I had no idea you were into that stuff."

"I wasn't really," Berg said. "I just started."

"Oh, okay…" Kenneth said. He appeared to be growing more and more confused. Berg knew it was confusing, knew it would take much more explaining for Kenneth to understand what had happened, but he didn't feel like telling the story.

"Well, nice running into you," Berg said.

"Yeah, you too," Kenneth said. "Let me know if you ever think about moving back to the city. My team is always looking for talent."

When they got their coffees they walked across the street to the park and sat on a bench. A woman in jeans and a T-shirt strolled past them, speaking Spanish into a large blue phone. An old man with a walker followed after her. There were two sliced-open tennis balls on the bottom of his walker and a purple plastic bag draped on top of it.

"Do you miss working at Cleanr?" Nell asked.

"Not at all," Berg said. "But I don't really care about what I'm doing now either."

"You're figuring it out."

"Am I? I'm pretty sure I'm just serving hummus on sailboats."

"You have to be patient, Berg. You'll find something. Maybe not in Talinas. But you'll find something."

The problem was he didn't know what he wanted. This did not seem to be something Nell struggled with. She knew what she cared about. It was part of what attracted him to her. But Berg's experience of the world had always been more plastic, more passive and coincidental. He had never been a man on a mission, exactly. He'd been a man who met a guy who had a friend who was doing this thing and sure, that seemed like an okay thing to do. That was certainly how he'd ended up with the Cleanr job. He didn't want to be that way and had an idea of himself as being something else. But what was he? He was twenty-seven years old. He had a lingering brain injury and he'd spent the last three years of his life working in the sales department of an antivirus startup and developing an opioid addiction. This was what he had become. Despite his near-perfect SAT score and his caring parents and the noble legacy of his grandfather, Rabbi Joel Rothman, may he rest in peace, Eli "Berg" Koenigsberg had, by all accounts, made nothing of himself.

When they finished their coffees, they walked over to the botanical gardens. There was some kind of event happening there that day. Several pianos had been placed throughout the gardens and anyone could sit down and play them. After a brief stroll, they stopped at the piano in the riparian woodland section. It had been placed between a coast live oak (*Quercus agrifolia*) and a hollyleaf cherry (*Prunus ilicifolia*). Berg sat down next to the cherry shrub and Nell took a seat at the piano. She began playing her own music, song after song, and slowly a crowd began to form. By the time she finished there were at least forty people standing there, hanging on her every word. She was that good.

CHAPTER 9

MANY PEOPLE IN MUIRE County believed that, if you lived in Talinas long enough, you would inevitably go crazy. They said that, before the town was built, the local indigenous people used the land for ceremonies to communicate with the spirit world. No one was supposed to live there or else they would become part spirit.

"She needs to move out to Alamere" was something people said to suggest that a person was losing her mind, that she should skip town before the spirits fully engulfed her. It was not exactly clear how and why people lost their minds, but it was agreed to be a general hazard of living in the area, like rogue waves or earthquakes.

Berg felt the myth had some credibility. Many of the town's residents seemed otherwise. There was Leanne Korver, for example, the local Pilates teacher, who believed in a complex pantheon of gods and was rumored to have stabbed a man in Santa Fe. And there was Greens, the son of Fred Perry, who owned the local hardware store. He refused to wear anything that wasn't bright green but other than that he was an entirely normal and sociable person. There were the Morrises, who believed they were Venutians and who had, at one time, convinced several other people in town that they were Venutians, too. And there was Woody, whom Berg had seen play guitar at the Tavern, but whom he met for the first time outside the supermarket.

It was Friday and Berg had stopped in to pick up some groceries for the weekend: a six-pack of beer, onions, bacon, some yogurt. He had a headache coming on, but it hadn't gotten bad yet. After he exited the store, he paused by the entrance to wedge the groceries into his backpack. He had to take the beers out of their package and stuff them individually in the backpack to get everything to fit. As he was doing this, someone called to him. He turned to see Woody, who was standing next to a newspaper rack, holding a blue package of cookies. He was short man, with black eyes and a curved red nose, like a turkey vulture.

"You're new around here," he said to Berg. "You want a cookie?"

"Sure," Berg said, swinging his backpack onto his shoulder.

"I've seen you at the Tavern before."

"Yeah, I remember you," Berg said.

"Woody Taglione," he said, holding out the package of cookies to Berg. "You'll see me around. I work all over town. Do a bit of everything. Ranching, construction, plumbing, diplomacy. By the way, you need a job? I know some guys that are trimming."

"No, I've got a job," Berg said, taking one of the cookies.

"Oh, okay. You come find me if you're looking, I live just over the road with my girl. Didn't grow up here, though. From Brooklyn originally. Greenpoint. Came out west in the '60s. Then I lived on a beach in Kauai for a few years. It was nice. Made jewelry, did acid about five hundred times. Hey, you wanna see something cool?"

"I guess."

"I'm not gonna show you unless you really want to see it."

"I want to see it."

"Like only if you really, really want to see it," he said, squinting at Berg.

"I do. I really want to see it," Berg said. And then he added: "Badly."

"Okay," Woody sighed. "If you insist."

Berg followed Woody down Main Street, backpack full of groceries, headache still there, stalking him, biding its time. They walked along 12, past the gift stores and the diner, and past the hill that had a small cross on it and the sign that said CROSSONAHILL.NET. The sun was a couple hours from setting, the weather still warm, the crickets louder than the frogs. At the point where 12 crossed Sausal Creek, Woody turned off the road and scrambled down a gully toward the water.

"Don't worry, I'm not going to murder you," he said. "Woulda done it by now if I was gonna murder you."

The creek down here was muddy and sluggish, thick with decaying leaves. On its banks were beer cans and candy wrappers and cigarette butts, a few tires and an orange cone. Woody brought Berg over to a manhole.

"I found this the other day when I was following a deer," he said. "This is probably from when the town was farther north, before the fire in the '50s." He opened the manhole and began climbing down its ladder, disappearing into the darkness. "Now," he called from below, his voice echoing slightly, "once you get to the fifth rung, you're going to have to leap to the left to avoid falling down this hole that leads to... well, I don't know where it leads to. Can't see it. But my point is that you want to jump to the left to avoid it. You got it?"

"I don't know..."

"Oh, it's safe. It's safe, man."

Berg climbed down the ladder until his hands were on the fifth rung. Directly below him was pitch-blackness but to his left he could see the outline of Woody's body. He jumped toward Woody and landed with one foot on Woody's ankle.

"Motherfuck," he said. "That's my bad ankle, man."

"I'm sorry."

"You know how I hurt this ankle?"

"No."

"Do you want to know?"

"I guess."

"I'm not gonna tell you unless you really want to know."

"I really want to know."

"Pickup basketball game at the rec center. Ted Burlington went and made a crossover and I fell sideways."

"That seems pretty common."

"I didn't say I'd hurt it in an uncommon way, did I?"

Woody pulled out a flashlight and trundled into the darkness. Berg had to hunch in order to avoid hitting his head on the ceiling but Woody was able to stand straight up. The air smelled like wet cement and garbage and rust. All around were sounds of dripping water, hollow and echoing. Berg could feel his headache getting worse, something about the air pressure or the smells down here. He took a bottle of ibuprofen from his bag and popped several pills, swallowed them without water.

After some time they arrived at a cavernous opening. Through the blackness Berg could make out the shape of several full-size, papier-mâché bodies. They were strung up by wire, hanging from the ceiling, slowly rotating in the air. Woody shined the flashlight on them one by one. Some of the bodies were grimacing and some were smiling. One appeared to be singing opera.

"You and me and whatever freak made these are the only people in the world who know about this," Woody said.

"I need to get out of here," Berg said.

"Wait, hang on a second," Woody said, lighting a cigarette. "Ain't we gonna drink those beers?"

CHAPTER 10

ONE DAY GARRETT ASKED Berg to help him drop off Vespucci's father's canoe at the local boatbuilder's shop. They loaded it onto the roof of his truck and drove north along the bay. It was autumn now and the grass that had been kept green by the summer fog had turned brown. Everything seemed brown: brown buildings, brown trees, brown cows. They listened to the local radio station as they drove, WMUR. The DJ was announcing different community events that week.

"Folks are needed on Sunday to help weed a patch of grass in the commons," he said. "Lot of weeds in the grass. Please help if you are able."

When they pulled up the driveway, Berg immediately recognized the house as one of the places he'd broken into. Down to the left was the old farmhouse he'd entered and, up to the right, there were two large barns. In the distance, behind the barns, Berg could make out what looked like a blue school bus. He didn't remember that school bus being here when he'd entered the farmhouse. He was staring at it, straining to remember whether he'd seen it before, when he realized that Garrett was saying his name.

"Dude," Garrett said. "Look alive. C'mon, let's go."

"Sorry... I just... I thought I might have been here before."

"You know Alejandro?"

"Who?"

"Alejandro Vega," Garrett said. "The boatbuilder."

"What? No."

"Or Uffa? You go to one of his bus shows some time?"

"Bus shows?"

"Yeah, he has musicians come and play on his bus. I went one night. Got totally shadracked. Stumbled home at 4 a.m."

"No, I've never been to one of those."

"Oh, well I can't say I recommend it. Bunch of freaks."

Instead of walking over to the farmhouse, Garrett led Berg up a short trail toward one of the old barns. A young man with a ponytail was standing by the door, smoking a spliff. He was wearing purple sweatpants, a purple sweatshirt, basketball shoes, and a fanny pack.

"What's up, Uffa?" Garrett said.

"'Sup, Garrett."

"This is Berg," Garrett said.

"Hi Berg."

"Sorry it took so long to get you this boat," Garrett said.

"Lots of bullshit happening. I won't go into it. Is Alejandro around?"

"Yeah, he's here but he's busy working. JC wants two new boats."

"How many have you built for him now?"

"I've lost count."

"You know, I've still never met that guy. Very mysterious."

"He's a good client," Uffa said.

"People say he's nuts. I mean, I've never met him so I don't know, but that's what people say."

Uffa didn't respond.

"Like, didn't he kill someone?" Garrett said. "In Mexico? I know he went postal on Teddy Kearns at the Western that one time."

Uffa stubbed out his spliff on the bottom of his boot. "Well, how 'bout we haul this boat inside?" he said.

The three men lifted the old canoe off the back of the truck and carried it into the barn. After they set it down on two sawhorses, Berg looked around. It was like being in some kind of cathedral. Tall ceilings and tall windows and boats hanging from the rafters, strung up by thick cords of rope, listing gently in the air. Everything shot through with columns of cold morning light, smelling of straw and saltwater and fresh sawdust. In the center of the shop there was a thirty-foot boat on blocks and, in the back, there was a loft. An older man was on his knees on the floor of the loft, staring at the ground, a pencil in his mouth. He was wearing jeans and sandals and a black turtleneck with holes in it. He did not look up from his work when they entered.

"Well, what do you think?" Garrett asked Uffa.

"There are no bleeding fasteners," Uffa said, circling the canoe. "And this crack that you were worried about is horizontal, not vertical. So we should be able to just put some bedding compound in there and it will be fine. We'll redo this rub strake for you, too."

"Great," Garrett said. "Thanks, Uffa. Hey, what happened to John? He's not working in the shop anymore?"

"Cut his hand on the table saw."

"Oh shit. You know, I thought his finger looked weird last time I saw him at the Western, but I wasn't sure if it had always been like that."

"Yeah, he lost a bit of his finger," Uffa said.

"I figured it might be something like that, but you never know. I met a girl in Willits who was born without a big toe. Some kind of deformity. Ran in the family. Several of them without big toes. Well, anyway." He looked around the shop, distracted. "We should get back to work. Mangini's really cracking the whip these days."

As Berg and Garrett walked back to the truck, a couple of dogs barked at them and then ran off toward some trees, distracted by a squirrel. In the distance, Berg saw a young girl running along the path down to the farmhouse, barefoot and tan, a fistful of blue flowers in her hand.

"I need to go back inside," Berg said.

"Why?" Garrett said.

"I'll just be a second."

"Okay," Garrett said, taking out his phone and beginning to flip through women on a dating app. "Hurry up."

Back in the barn, Berg found Uffa leaning over the canoe, picking at a piece of caulking near the stern.

"Oh hey," Uffa said.

"Hi. I was wondering if you guys need any help now, because Tom's hand was hurt and all."

"John?"

"Right, John's hand, and I was thinking that maybe… I mean I don't know how to do anything, really… but…"

"You'd have to talk to ask Alejandro about this," Uffa said. He led Berg across the shop and up the stairs to the loft.

"Ale," Uffa said. "This is Berg. He's interested in becoming an apprentice."

Now that Berg was up on the floor of the loft, he could see what Alejandro was working on. It was a big sketch of a boat, precise and elegant. The sketch was drawn on multiple pieces of plywood, which had been painted white, and it ran the entire length of the barn. The old man looked up from the drawing and took off his glasses. His eyes were a muddy blue, the color of pond water.

"You would like to be an apprentice?" he asked.

"Yes," Berg said. "I mean, I think so. I don't really know what that means."

"It means you work here four days a week for free for the next month and then, if you like the work and we like each other, I begin to pay a stipend for the next two years. And you can live in that cubby back there, if you like."

Berg turned around and saw that there was a triangular door at the far end of the loft floor.

"That would be great," he said.

"Very good then," Alejandro said. He stood up, hobbled over to Berg, and shook his hand. He smelled like coffee and sweet tobacco. "I hope you find the work rewarding," he said. "It's not for everyone, and that's okay. If you don't like it, you don't like it. It's no problem."

"Okay," Berg said, desperately hoping he would like it.

"You'll start next week."

Berg walked outside and got into Garrett's truck. As they drove back to Fernwood, he watched the bay on his right. Small coves and reedy beaches, a light fog approaching, wolf-colored and wet. He did some quick calculus to determine whether or not he would be able to afford the apprenticeship. If he kept working at Fernwood a few days a week, he could probably get by. Then he thought about how he'd broken into what he now assumed was Alejandro's house, months ago. He thought about all the photos of boats and the oilskin map. He thought about the Lortabs and the amulet and how he'd taken a shit in the bathroom. But these memories were too shameful, too sad. He pushed them out of his mind, far out of his mind, to the extent that, weeks later, he was not sure if they were even real.

CHAPTER 11

FOR THE FIRST FEW days of his apprenticeship, Berg didn't do anything but sharpen. The key to good woodworking, Alejandro said, and boatbuilding in particular, is having sharp tools. And the key to sharpening tools, he explained, is patience and awareness. If you did not maintain balanced strokes against the stone, the edge of the blade would begin to round. On the first day, Alejandro gave Berg a brief lesson in sharpening and then he set him loose.

Berg's first task was to get the flat end of the chisel entirely level. You did this by rubbing the back of the chisel against the water stones, applying pressure to the front edge of chisel, where it was likely to lift up. From there, you gave the beveled side of the blade an angle, stabilizing the chisel with both hands. After every few strokes, you would dip the blade in a plastic tub of water and hold it up to the light to examine it. It was crucial to keep the blade at the same angle the whole time. If your hands shifted position, you would begin sharpening at a different angle and the blade would become dull.

Berg's progress was slow. He had always had shaky hands—his friends in high school had made fun of him for it—and he couldn't figure out how to keep the handle of the chisel stable as he sharpened. All it took was the tiniest twitch and then he had made a bad stroke and he basically had to start all over. His mind would wander, too. He'd be paying attention to the strokes, placing them carefully and accurately, and then he'd begin to think about something else—if Nell was really going to get a dog, as she'd said on the phone the other day; how he owed his brother a call; how he'd left the acetone uncapped in the toolshed at Fernwood—and he would make another bad stroke and have to backpedal.

After the first couple of days he managed to produce a few moderately sharp chisels and Alejandro gave him a plane blade to work on. Uffa had just returned from a trip to Oakland and it was the first day the two of them were working together at the same time. Berg sharpened the blade Alejandro had given him for about an hour and, at one point, he got a pretty good angle going and he began to wonder if he was finished. He looked at the blade in the light, as Alejandro had demonstrated, and tried to determine if it was perfectly flat. He wasn't sure. He decided to walk over to Alejandro and show him.

Alejandro was working a big piece of lumber with an adze.

He set down the adze and held Berg's blade to the light, chest heaving.

"No," he said.

And then he picked up the adze and went back to work. Berg returned to the bench and continued with his strokes. Twenty minutes later he walked back to Alejandro to show him the blade. He was pretty confident that he'd done it right and, if he hadn't, he wanted Alejandro to show him what was wrong. He presented Alejandro with the blade and Alejandro showed him how, in the upper right corner, there was a slight difference of color, indicating that the blade was not ready. He put down his adze and looked at Berg.

"When was the last time you got lost in a thing?"

"What do you mean?"

"When was the last time you were working so hard that you forgot what you were doing?"

"I don't know."

"You're very punctual, aren't you?"

It wasn't easy to answer the question. Before he'd become an addict, yes, he was punctual. Berg said nothing.

"You're punctual because you're always thinking about the next place you're going to be."

Berg bristled, but a part of him also knew Alejandro was right. Alejandro was meeting the non-stoned version of Berg, the tense, anxious, calculating version. This version was punctual, he was right. This version had risen through the ranks at Cleanr, always hungry, always looking to prove himself, hurtling toward eventual burnout. Of course, at Cleanr, he had been doing something that didn't matter to him. Now he wanted to get it right.

"It's not your fault," Alejandro continued. "Stop thinking about the result. Stop wanting it to be over right away and I promise everything will go better."

The key was not even sharpening the blade, he told Berg. The key was staying completely in the room with what he was doing. Berg said nothing, returned to the sharpening stone, irritated and hurt. He tried to sharpen again, but now he was even more distracted. His mind wandered back to what Alejandro had said, wandered away toward something else. He missed a few strokes and found himself once again with a rounded blade. Frustrated, he put down the chisel and took out his phone, checked his social media. Photo of a stack of art books. Photo of someone's toast. Photo of Nell drinking coffee. Uffa noticed him on his phone and walked over.

"The sharpening takes a long time," he said. "You'll get it, though. When I started I didn't know how to do any of this stuff. It's good to learn it. Having sharp tools makes everything easier."

"Thanks."

"What are you doing after we finish?"

"I don't know."

"Want to come hang out on the bus?"

Uffa had bought the bus five years ago, from a river rafting company in Truckee. He had recently installed an atrium on the roof, he told Berg, because he was tired of hunching. The atrium ran down the center of the roof, like scales on the back of a dragon. Inside the bus he had added a pepperwood cabinet and a fir desk. There was a jar of weed on the floor and a VHS of *Jurassic Park* and two guitars. Beneath his bed were several milk crates full of clothes and a pile of notebooks.

"Trying to write one poem a day for all of September," Uffa said.

Last summer, Uffa told Berg, he had taken the bus up to Washington with several musicians. They all lived in a warehouse in Oakland, along with a couple of poets and a filmmaker and a visual artist. Most of them worked in the service industry, waiting tables or bartending. Uffa moved in and out of a room in the warehouse and the bus, depending on how much money he had at the moment. When he was living on the bus, he usually posted up next to the dog park that was around the corner from the warehouse. The dog park was a thin strip of fenced-in land and, every Sunday, Uffa served coffee and hot chocolate to the people who used it. This was part of the ongoing public relations campaign that he hoped would prevent someone from reporting his illegal residence. For the past couple of months he'd been in Talinas, helping Alejandro. He usually worked with Alejandro for about half of the year.

"I come up here," he said, "earn a few survival tickets, and then head back to the dog park."

Alejandro had most recently called him up here because he was working on a big boat for a drug dealer named JC. This was the boat that was currently sitting on blocks in the center of the shop. It was called the *Alma*. Apparently JC commissioned a lot of boats from Alejandro. Uffa said he used them to pick up weed in Mexico. The boats were both a form of transportation and a decoy. Most DEA agents expected product to come up from Mexico in little fishing boats, not wooden sailboats.

"It's not as sketchy as it sounds," Uffa said. "I mean, JC is sketchy. That guy is certifiably sketchy. But me and Alejandro, we're normal. Well, Alejandro is a genius, but he's mostly normal. Here, come look at this."

Uffa walked over to his desk and picked up a framed painting. It depicted a scene at some kind of Islamic palace, with men playing strange instruments and carrying bowls of fruit. The work was insanely detailed, full of bright, pure color.

"Alejandro taught himself how to do this," Uffa said. "Persian miniature painting. Can you believe that? I mean, the skill here… it's off the charts. He thought this painting was bad, though. He was going to throw it out. I convinced him to save it, to let me have it."

Berg sat down at the desk and inspected the painting. The desk was covered with papers and magazine clippings and a few dirty glasses that seemed, at one point, to have contained green smoothies. Uffa lit a spliff and the room filled with sweet, skunky smoke. He continued to muse while Berg examined the painting.

"You know, you came here at a good time. Business has been strong recently. We're getting more JC commissions than ever. And JC pays well. I mean, we're not rich. You won't get rich working here, that's for sure. But you'll learn a lot of skills. Some of Alejandro's apprentices go on to become carpenters or cab-inetmakers, and that can be okay money. Don't get into chairs, though. No one makes money on chairs."

The closer Berg looked at the painting, the more he saw. There was a cat curled up on a rug, a man weighing some kind of precious metal on a scale, herbs drying, tiny golden keys, and several donkeys. It was ambitious, accomplished, not the kind of thing you would just throw away.

"Last apprentice we had didn't make it," Uffa continued. "Oh, I told you about him, actually. Garrett asked about him. He ended up cutting his finger. John Pressey. I'm glad he quit. I mean, I'm sorry he cut his finger and all but I'm glad he quit. Didn't really like hanging out with him. Had a stressy vibe. He was always talking about how he couldn't balance his art life with his work life and going on about some existential crisis and I was just like, 'Man, I don't need any more of that shit in my life.' Between myself and everyone at the warehouse… I've got plenty. We don't need any more of that around here."

Uffa opened a bag of walnuts, took a handful, and held out the bag to Berg.

"You want some of these?" he said. "Brain food."

Berg set down the painting and took a few walnuts. He motioned to the donkeys in the painting.

"My grandfather was really interested in donkeys," he said. "Well, donkeys as symbols in Jewish literature. He thought they represented *yezerah,* the aspect of our physical nature that separates us from God. All of the great Jewish leaders—Moses, Abraham—were depicted holding the reins of a donkey, and this, my grandfather said, was meant to symbolize their mastery over their own inner beasts. They could not practice *tikun olam,* the healing of the world, until they mastered their own *yezerah.*"

"Ride the donkey," Uffa said. "I like that. Is that what you were doing before you came out here? Studying Jewish stuff?"

"No, no," Berg said. "I sold antivirus software."

"I see," Uffa said. "Another digital refugee."

"I'm free now, though," Berg said. "I made it out."

"Damn right. Now you can do whatever you want."

"I want to build boats," Berg said, popping a walnut in his mouth.

"Oh, you're gonna learn about that," Uffa said.

He walked over to the desk and ashed his spliff on a small plate.

"You're gonna be up to your eyes in boats," he said. "Catboats, tugboats, dories, cutters, skiffs. I get bored of it some of the time, to be honest. Like, why don't we try making a car? Or a dishwasher? Or a robot cat, you know? Shake things up. But Alejandro's always boats, boats, boats. You won't want for boats, man. You found the boat king."

CHAPTER 12

BERG CUT DOWN HIS hours at Fernwood. He worked there only two days a week now and spent the rest of his time at Alejandro's. Even if there was nothing to do in the shop, Berg would hang out in the farmhouse and talk to Alejandro, or whoever was around. At first Berg felt like he was intruding, but Alejandro made him feel welcome.

"Do you want to stay for dinner, Berg?" he'd ask, eyes twinkling.

Alejandro and his wife, Rebecca, lived in the main farmhouse with their two teenage sons, Hal and Sandy. Their daughters, who were older, lived on different parts of the property. Lizzie was married to a Dutch man named Jens, and she had given birth to Alejandro's only grandchild, Tess. They lived in a cabin down by the water. Marie, Alejandro's other daughter, lived by herself, baked sourdough bread, and on occasion helped out her father in the boat shop. Alejandro never would have said it, but Berg could tell she was his favorite child.

Berg guessed that Alejandro was around sixty-five years old. Every morning, he woke at sunrise and took a walk through the woods. When he returned from his walk, he had toast, eggs, and cowboy coffee, and read the paper all the way through. Uffa, Rebecca, and his children rose around this time, and joined him in the kitchen for breakfast. There was a jovial atmosphere to the farmhouse in the mornings, with Rebecca and all of the children discussing the farm-related work that needed to be done that day. On any given morning, the generator needed to be fixed, the irrigation in the tomato patch repaired, the animals fed, the goats' toenails clipped, the bread made, the cheese made, the sausage made, the cows milked, the fence by the chicken run mended, the pear trees pruned and inspected for blight, the soil temperature recorded, and someone needed to go into town to buy a five-gallon bucket.

Alejandro said he was part Chilean, part Hawaiian, and part "something else." He'd grown up in Tahiti and California and his father had made his living chartering tourists back and forth from the West Coast to Tahiti on a schooner named *Hoku Lewa*. There was a large black-and-white photo of this boat in the shop. It hung above the workbench, next to a photo of Uffa and Alejandro from many years ago. In that photo, the two men were standing in front of the ribcage of some small boat, both of them in overalls. Uffa looked very young in the photo. He couldn't have been more than eighteen years old.

The boat shop was a large, airy place. It was not entirely disordered but you could not say it was orderly, either. There were miscellaneous cans of turpentine and linseed oil, stacks of black locust and pepperwood and cedar, old paper coffee cups full of fasteners and bolts, and hundreds of tools, some of them in better shape than others. Several dogs came in and out of the shop, and Berg's favorite dog was named Swallow. She was a black-grey mutt with long eyelashes and a runny snout. During the first week of his apprenticeship, she ate a dead squirrel and it made her horribly sick. Berg found her behind the shop vomiting, but she seemed to be in good spirits. In between each heave she would look up at Berg, entirely unrepentant.

I'd do it again, she seemed to be saying. *I loved eating the squirrel and I'd do it all again.*

Berg learned that many people in Talinas believed Alejandro to be mentally ill. One day he ran into Joe Leggett in town, for example, and told him he was apprenticing with Alejandro. He hadn't seen Leggett since he stopped going to the Tavern.

"Good luck with that," Leggett said. "That guy's a quack."

It was true that Alejandro was strange. His mind was borderless and kinetic. He'd sit down and talk to his six-year-old granddaughter for two hours and become entirely absorbed in the child's world. His yard was littered with broken-down cars and other detritus. Shortly after Berg met him, he became interested in pasteurizers, and designed and built his own portable pasteurizer for Rebecca to use in the field. After that he began carving Elizabethan lutes. He would stay in the shop after hours, working on these lutes that he didn't know how to play.

But Berg never doubted Alejandro's sanity because the first thing he'd seen was his work: his first experiences with Alejandro revolved around building, and everything Alejandro did matched, everything fit. He was a master with hand tools and his intellectual horsepower was astonishing. He would stay up late into the night, smoking hand-rolled cigarettes and drinking coffee and looking at lines. Berg would try to keep up with him for a few hours but then he'd fatigue.

"The lines of American fishing boats are high art," Alejandro said. "Americans are strange. We do certain things that are unfathomable, like sit in traffic. To me this is evidence of mass psychosis, all of these people sitting in traffic. But the lines of American boats are both beautiful and practical."

As much as Berg liked spending time with Alejandro, he felt inferior in his company. Alejandro was so confident and intelligent, his daily existence so full of life, that Berg felt intimidated. Alejandro never stopped investigating and questioning, and Berg, unfamiliar with even the basics of some of the issues Alejandro was exploring, struggled to keep up. About 30 percent of the time he didn't understand what Alejandro was talking about, but he just kept hanging on, kept listening, like a foreigner trying to learn a new language.

Much of Alejandro's work relied on sensory intelligence. He was able, for example, to determine the exact moisture content of a piece of wood by smelling it. This was important because wood changed shape as it dried. If you did not accurately determine moisture content, you might end up with a boat that, after a couple of years, had large gaps between its planks. Various species of wood had widely different structural properties and dried at different rates.

"You see," Alejandro would say, holding a cut of white oak to Berg's nose. "You must know the smells for each wood."

The way the wood was cut mattered, too. Most lumber was flat-sawn, but Alejandro would quarter-saw his lumber because it gave him more pieces of wood with vertical grain. This type of wood was less likely to shrink or develop checks.

"When a tree dries," Alejandro said, "it is opening from the pith. Its rings are trying to flatten out. So a piece of wood with highly curved rings, a piece with horizontal grain, is going to move more than a piece of wood with flat rings, or vertical grain. You must anticipate this. You must always be thinking about how the wood will change with time."

Alejandro's professorial style was highly improvisational. After discussing the differences between vertical and horizontal grains, he might point to the floorboards of the shop, show Berg how they were horizontal grain and how they had checked. From there he might explain how there was adobe under the floor of the shop, which would lead to a discussion of California's geology, which would segue into a commentary on the exceptionally hot lava of Kilauea, and move from there to a story about hula, the slow form of hula that his mother had practiced in Tahiti, which was distinct from the more common, touristic version of the dance—all of this concluding, somehow, with a contemplation of the cello as an instrument, its merits and deficiencies. It was dizzying, but it was always interesting.

One day, when Berg was caulking the *Alma*, a reporter came into the shop. He said he was looking for Alejandro and Berg told him that Alejandro was out by the mouth fishing for herring. It was November and the herring run stretched from one end of the bay to the other, a forty-foot-wide river of shimmering silver.

"Do you know when he'll be back?"

"I don't."

"No idea at all?"

Berg yelled over to Uffa, who was at the other end of the

shop, cutting blocks for the *Alma* and soaking them in linseed oil. He said he didn't know either.

"I'm sorry," Berg said to the reporter. "We don't know when he'll be back."

"I want to ask him about Szerbiak," the reporter said. "I drove all the way out here." He was wearing a dress shirt and glasses and he had a sweater tied around his neck.

"The novelist?" Berg asked.

"Yes, of course the novelist," the man said, irritated.

"I'm sorry," Berg said. "If you leave your name and number, I'll pass it to him."

When Alejandro came home, Berg told him about the man who had stopped by. Alejandro seemed disturbed, wanted to know what the man looked like. Berg described him, and then he asked Alejandro if he'd known Szerbiak.

"I went to college with him," Alejandro replied.

"That's so cool. His work is amazing."

"It was cool for a while but I'm done with that scene. It was a dead end. The whole scene was a dead end." He picked up a wooden mallet and began to caulk alongside Berg. "If that man comes back," he said, "tell him I don't live here."

CHAPTER 13

WINTER IN TALINAS WAS a great reawakening. The heavy rains brought out the ferns and the mosses, and the fruit orchards stood knee-deep in grass. In the hills the wild mustard grew tall and yellow, and the bees emerged from their cells to pollinate the buttercups. Around the bay, the trails became so overgrown that you felt, when you walked along them, as if you were wading through a shallow pool.

During winter, Alejandro heated the shop with two wood stoves, which he fed with scrap wood from their boat projects. He had connected a pipe to one of the wood stoves and run it to the shop bathroom, which allowed them to have steam showers. While most of his work came from JC, whom Berg had still not met, Alejandro also did some repair work and took commissions from other people in town, usually for small boats, dories or canoes. That fall, for example, they replaced several planks on a fishing boat and they also repaired Vespucci's canoe.

Alejandro helped out on the farm, too, but that was primarily Rebecca's domain. She ran the whole thing herself, growing vegetables and raising cows, goats, and chickens. Her gardens were colorful and overflowing. There were medicinal herbs and native grasses, as well as a wide variety of produce. Green beans and chilies and zucchinis. Acorn squash and yellow squash and winter squash. She liked squash.

Rebecca had grown up in Santa Margarita, down south. She was a strong, solid woman, her skin dark from days in the sun. She dressed simply, in jeans and white shirts that she sewed herself. Her glasses were round and thick and, as far as Berg could tell, she never lied. She was a born farmer, had thousands of different projects all over the property. But of all her labors, she seemed to take most joy in caring for the animals. And of all the animals, she seemed to like the geese best.

Her granddaughter, Tess, was also enamored with the geese. Apparently, last year, one of the geese had given birth to goslings, whom Tess had been permitted to adore for several days before they were sold off, to her dismay. This subject came up often around the house and Berg could tell that, for Tess, the loss of the goslings had been a great tragedy.

Tess was six years old. She was something of a feral child, spending every day outdoors, hunting lizards and climbing trees and building small dams out of rocks and sticks. Like her grandfather, she was highly inquisitive. She was always asking questions, always trying to solve some new puzzle. Her uncles, Sandy and Hal, liked to take her out in the little dhow that they'd built. They called it the *Wildcat*, and they'd often sail it over to Horse Island, pretending, with Tess, that they were explorers discovering the bay for the first time.

Sandy and Hal spent their days at school, but when they came home, they helped out around the farm, or looked after Tess. Whenever Berg spoke with them, they were always in a good mood: bright, mannerly teenagers, at peace with their place in the world. They understood that their life was not a common one, but it did not trouble them. They were proud to be Vegas, proud to go to school as representatives of that strange family that lived off the l and wore funny handmade clothes.

One night, Nell and Berg had dinner with Alejandro's whole family and a couple of their friends from town, Morty Weisenstein, the WMUR radio talk show host, and his partner, Jacob, who was a professor at a state university. Uffa didn't join them. He was out on a date with a girl he'd just started seeing, Demeter.

After their meal, the dinner party walked over to the shop to inspect the *Alma*. The boat was nearing completion, would soon be ready for its launch. Morty commented on the beauty of the boat's transom and Alejandro explained that its dimensions were very similar to another boat he'd designed.

"It's right up here in the rafters, actually," he said.

Using a block and tackle, Alejandro lowered the boat so they could inspect it. The transom did resemble *Alma*'s: it was slanted and curved, cut from pepperwood. This boat was significantly smaller, however, with a bold sheer and a high bow. It was called the *Coot*.

"Uffa built one of these boats himself," Alejandro explained.

"Took him a whole year. But then he and his friends had this idea to stage a Viking funeral as some kind of art project."

"No, Ale," Rebecca said, "it was for a scene in a movie. They were making a short film."

"Oh, that's right," Alejandro said. "Well, in any case, they filled the boat with straw and set it on fire, out on the bay."

"Isn't that illegal?" Jacob asked.

"Yes," Alejandro said. "Uffa does insane things like this every once a while."

"He has an artistic sensibility," Rebecca said.

Berg circled the *Coot*. He wanted so badly to be able to build something that beautiful, but he wasn't even close. Alejandro had first started working an adze in Tahiti—standing in gallon buckets to protect his legs from stray cuts—when he was eight years old. Berg wanted to be exactly like him, to possess his skill and patience and calm self-reliance. But they were fundamentally different people, with different minds and different backgrounds, and every once in a while, as Berg was striving to understand what Alejandro understood, the vast gulf between the two of them became vividly clear, and a great, quiet pain rose up in him. He would never be Alejandro. So what was he trying to become?

The dinner party hung around the shop for a while, drinking wine, and then Berg and Nell walked home. Back at Mimi's, Berg made a pot of tea and brought it into the living room. Nell was leaning against the far wall, across from the desk, stretching her calves. She was always stretching at unusual times, in unusual places.

"That isn't caffeinated, is it?" Nell asked.

"No."

"The other night I went out for Chinese food and I was just gulping down all this tea, not realizing it was caffeinated, and it kept me up until 4 a.m. For a while I kept trying to fall asleep but then I was just like, okay, this isn't happening, and I went into the living room and read all these letters by my great aunt that I'd been meaning to look through. Her father was a private investigator in New York. Have I ever told you that? I didn't really find anything in the letters yet. It's mostly just gossip. Like, 'Did you see the rakish angle of Eleanor's hat at the races last week?' That kind of thing."

Nell finished her stretch and started for the couch but something caught her eye. She approached the desk instead.

"Have you been painting, Berg?"

"Kind of," he said. He set the tea down on the coffee table and followed her over to the desk. "They're really bad," he said, picking up one of the paintings.

"They're not so bad," she said. "Is this, like, an abstract portrait?"

"It's a mountain."

"Okay, yeah, sure," she said. "I see that. Mountain. Very cool."

"Those are two little coyotes right there," Berg said.

"Oh yep, got the coyotes."

"I saw this painting that Alejandro made... I know they're not good."

"They're not great, but it's cool. I'm glad you're doing it. It's better than playing that role-playing video game on your phone when you get home from work."

Berg set the painting down and walked over to the couch. Nell followed. He poured them both cups of tea, wrinkled his nose.

"I get frustrated by Alejandro's talent sometimes," he said.

"At painting?"

"At painting, at boatbuilding. Mainly boatbuilding. His intelligence is far greater than mine. That is clear to me. And seeing it so clearly… I don't know. It makes me wonder if this whole thing is futile, if I'm ever going to be able to do the things he does."

Nell cupped her mug of tea with two hands, blew ripples into it.

"It's hard when you meet a master," she said. "I felt that way about my old guitar teacher."

"Half the time I can't even follow what he's talking about," Berg said. "And then, when I can, when I actually understand the task, there's a good chance I won't be able to execute it properly. That's the most frustrating thing, and it happens all the time. I'll know how something should be done, but I can't necessarily do it. My understanding always outstrips my skills."

Nell took a sip of the tea.

"What makes you think that will ever change?" she said.

CHAPTER 14

TO BERG, THE SHRIEKS and yells of the coyotes sounded like a human party. A party that had been crashed by kids from another town and was, perhaps, about to get out of control. When the sun went down in Talinas, wherever you were, you could hear them. But you could never tell how close they were. Berg had seen a few of them during the day, while walking around the bay. They seemed watchful but relaxed, like rangers patrolling the county.

The coyotes sounded loudest from Woody's porch, where Berg often found himself after work. Uffa, it turned out, was close friends with Woody, and around 5 p.m. he and Berg would usually go over to Woody's house and sit on the porch and drink a couple of beers. While they drank, the coyotes would bark and shriek and Woody would complain about this, insist that there used to be fewer coyotes, that things in the neighborhood were quieter then.

Woody lived up by the gas station, in an area that was known locally as the Plains. It was situated on the northern edge of the town and it was considerably more down-at-the-heel. A couple of single-story apartment complexes but mostly mobile homes, parked haphazardly on an expanse of thistle and grass. There were clotheslines strung between trees and rusted beach chairs and abandoned crab traps. Almost everyone except for Woody and his girlfriend, Claudette, was Latino. One of the mobile homes had been converted into a taco truck and Berg, Uffa, and Woody ate there often. Woody usually ordered seven tacos and two Modelo Negras. Most of the time he didn't finish the last taco. Sometimes he didn't finish the last two tacos.

"Why don't you order fewer tacos to begin with?" Uffa said.

"I was raised in a home of scarcity," Woody said. "I have instincts. I can't help myself."

Like many people in Talinas, Woody seemed to have several different jobs. Some days he milked Al Garther's cows and other days he would be weeding Jillian Lewis' front yard. On occasion, if they were short-handed, he washed dishes at the Station House. He also had his standing gig at the Tavern on Friday nights where he'd sing his deer songs.

Sometimes, instead of sitting on the porch, they would go inside and watch Woody's favorite show, *Salvage Kings*. In one episode, the main guy salvaged a large fan and valves from a mill in South Carolina. In another episode, they built a coffee table out of an old factory cart. Woody was always talking about things he might potentially salvage around Talinas.

"One day I'm going to head up there and take that old windmill from Gary Larson's dairy and hang it on the front of the trailer. I'm also interested in that pile of dowel rods next to Daryl Shapton's driveway."

"What do you want with a pile of dowel rods?" Uffa asked.

"I have yet to decide."

Woody told stories about his past but they were often disjointed and difficult to follow, like an avant-garde novel. Over time, Berg began to piece together a sense of his biography. Woody had run away from home at sixteen and moved to Chicago to join an anarchist collective, where he'd met a man named Treehouse John.

"We were doing a lot of graffiti and stuff," Woody said, "and we issued political manifestos every once in a while. But honestly, most of it was just partying. By 1969, it was obvious nothing was gonna change so that's when me and John decided to go to Hawaii."

In Hawaii they lived in a tent on the beach and sold jewelry in town. After a few years, they returned to California, strung out and broke, their skin golden like French fries. They both moved to Talinas and became involved with a drug rehabilitation program that turned out to be a cult.

"We were fooled, I'll admit it," Woody said. "But many people were fooled. Like 30 percent of this town are former members."

"This is the thing with the Morrises?" Berg asked. "The people who thought they were Venutians?"

"No, no, no," Woody said. "That was only a handful of people. This was a totally different thing. Much bigger. Like I said, 30 percent of the town are former members. Maybe even 40. Who knows? They don't do polling on this type of stuff so we'll never know but it could be as high as 40."

"When did you know it was a cult?" Berg asked.

"When everyone shaved their heads. That's when I got out. One day they were like: 'Warren shaved his head and now everyone else is shaving their head!'" Woody tapped his temple. "That's when I thought, Aha, cult."

On occasion Woody's neighbor Diego would come over and hang out with the three of them. He was six foot six and two hundred fifty pounds but he always drank Coronitas, the little seven-ounce beers, because he said they stayed cold and carbonated the whole time you drank them. Diego was the manager on Al Garther's ranch. He was the one who helped Woody secure jobs around the county. His wife, Esme, kept several birds as pets. A few months ago, Woody had found an injured snowy plover and brought it to their house and Esme had nursed it back to health.

"She fed it… What did she feed it?" Woody said.

"Mashed-up crickets," Diego replied.

"Mashed crickets," Woody said, wonder in his voice. "Mashed crickets, that's right. And then all of a sudden it was better. Incredible. She's a genius, that woman."

Woody was in his early sixties. He lived with his girlfriend, Claudette, who usually came home late in the evening and joined them on the porch. She was a little younger than Woody, with brown hair and warm, hooded eyes. She had come to Talinas in the '90s after the two of them started dating. They had met at the Six Flags in Vallejo, where Claudette used to work.

"I was a big fan of Six Flags back in the day," Woody said. "Big, big fan. Addicted, some would have said, no doubt, but look at me now: do you see me at Six Flags these days? No. So I think… What I'm trying to say is I was not addicted. I have a passion for the place. That I will grant you."

Woody often spoke about his friend Leonard, although Berg had yet to meet him. He claimed that they were going to make a documentary about Leonard's family for Shark Week this year.

"Leonard has been saying that every year since Shark Week started," Claudette said. "Which was like, what, 1994?"

"Doesn't mean this year won't be the year," Woody said. "Leonard thinks it will. I think so, too."

"Leonard's father is Sharkman," Claudette explained to Berg.

"Who?" Berg said.

"You don't know who Sharkman is?" Woody exclaimed. "Sharkman!" he said, and raised his eyebrows at Berg.

"I don't know who that is," Berg said.

"Sharkman is a guy who studies great white sharks out at the Slide Islands," Claudette said. "Been doing it for many years. He's famous around the county because he has survived over three shark attacks."

"Some say he himself is a shark," Woody added.

"He uses a piece of rug cut out to look like a seal to lure the sharks toward his boat," Claudette said. "When he was younger he would swim around out there but then he got attacked three times so he stopped that."

"He's getting honored at the annual Dance Palace thing this year," Woody said. "He's almost retired. I want to go but I've been unofficially banned from the event."

"What about your ban is unofficial?" Claudette asked.

"I haven't signed a contract."

"You don't need to sign a contract. They banned you," Claudette said. Then she turned to Berg: "Last year Woody got too drunk at the Dance Palace award ceremony and grabbed the mic and started lecturing everyone about how there are aliens living among us."

"A lot of people agreed with me, for the record. They came up to me afterward and said, 'Woody, I found your comments sensible and instructive.'"

"The problem was more with the yelling and the profanity," Claudette said.

"Well, people need to wake up," Woody said. "People need to open their eyes."

CHAPTER 15

ONE EVENING, BERG AND Uffa were sitting on Woody's porch drinking beer and Berg mentioned that he was still working at Fernwood two days a week.

"Oh, I didn't realize you worked there," Woody said. "You said you were doing maintenance so I assumed you were down at Vlasic's Boat Yard."

"No, Fernwood."

"So you know Garrett then?" Woody said.

"Yeah, how do you know him?"

"He used to work at the restaurant with Claudette. He was

one of the shuckers but then he sliced open his hand real bad. Or maybe he sliced someone else's hand? I can't remember. Someone was sliced. Anyway Conotic fired him."

Woody asked Berg if he would talk to Garrett about getting him some work.

"You think they'd hire me?" Woody said. "I know they've got a ton of money up there. I'll do whatever, man. Ask Diego. I'm not picky. I'll wax the boss's car, whatever. Detail that shit. I don't care."

Berg meant to talk to Garrett about Woody the following day, but he didn't have time before their charter began. It was an early-morning trip, an ash-scattering out by Horse Island. The client was a winemaker from Napa named George Wagner. He was in his fifties and he was accompanied by his wife and two children. The whole time they motored toward the island, George Wagner talked about how much his mother loved Horse Island. She'd grown up in Muire County, in Western Valley, and she'd sailed on the bay as a young girl. Garrett asked a lot of questions about the mother as they motored. This was something he would never do on a trip that was not an ash-scattering, but he was very respectful during ash-scatterings. He took an interest in the deceased and he rang a solemn bell seven times when the ashes were poured over the gunwales, always on the leeward side, to prevent the ashes from blowing back into the client's face. Berg found this side of Garrett endearing and, in a strange way, he looked forward to ash-scatterings.

But today, Garrett had fucked up. As they neared Horse Island, Garrett said what he always said, which was: "Let me know when and where you'd like to begin the ceremony for your mother."

Unfortunately, it was not the man's mother who had died. It was his sister. Garrett blanched when he learned this and remained silent for the rest of the charter. When they got back to the dock, Garrett checked the text message Mangini had sent him about the charter, hoping to find that Mangini was responsible for the mistake and not him, but the information was clear:

"Horse Island Charter. Dock time: 11:00 a.m. Four passengers. Client name: Wagner. Ash-scattering for client's sister, Jane Englander."

After Berg and Simon finished putting the boat to bed, Berg walked over to Garrett's office. He found him squeezing a stress ball, flipping through a motorcycle parts catalogue. On his desk were timesheets and paper coffee cups and a book called *How to Win Every Argument*.

"Do you think I'm a bad person?" Garrett said, the moment Berg walked into his office. "Am I bad?"

"What?"

"You know what I mean, Berg," Garrett said. He had yet to look up from the motorcycle parts catalogue.

"Are you talking about that charter?" Berg said. "I wouldn't worry about it, Garrett. Everyone messes up."

"When I was thirteen I stole a pager from the Circuit City in Pine Gulch," Garrett said. "Does that change your opinion?" He was looking at Berg now.

"A pager?"

"When I was fourteen I convinced my little sister that my mom was going to give her up for adoption. Send her to Thailand. Then, when I was fifteen, I pantsed this kid in front of the whole class. His name was JBaum. Well that was his nickname. He was the easiest target. Everyone went after him. Had this skinny little body and this really big head. A few days later I started a rumor that JBaum was having a party and I looked up his address in the directory and put it on a bunch of fliers and plastered them around school."

"Did people go to his house?"

"Some, yes, and his father turned them away at the door. Or so I'm told. I didn't go."

"Where is JBaum now?"

"He's around. Pours concrete with Freddie Moltisanti."

"Who?"

"The kid who lived in a cave. But the point is that JBaum and I never talked about it. And I imagine he still hates my guts. And I was thinking, when I saw these school shootings happening, I was thinking: I'm the guy that would've teased the shooter. I'm the guy that would've driven him over the edge and the first guy he'd come looking for when he barged into the school."

"Just because you teased someone doesn't mean you deserve to get shot..."

"I get to thinking about death sometimes, you know? Like, what will it be like? When I'm there, lying in some hospital bed, waiting to leave the world. Or I've got a bullet in my gut. Or I'm drowning in the bay, choking on salt water. I don't believe in God. Used to, but don't anymore. My mom believed in God till the day she died. That's how she explained all the shitty things my dad would do. 'The Lord has a plan for us,' she would say and I would think: the Lord is really planning things poorly. This is the best plan the Lord came up with? Why didn't the Lord just have us win the lottery? Well, we did try and win the lottery. Bought Scratchers like every weekend. But you see what I'm saying? I just couldn't make it fit together. I lost God and he never came back—or she—I know you're one of these politically correct guys. You probably think God could've been a woman. I've heard these theories. It seems unlikely to me, but what do I know? The point is that I'll get to thinking about death and the possibility that there's nothing beyond this world and I'll wonder, What did I do with my time? Why did I ever cause anyone pain? But I have, and I continue to, even when I don't mean to, like today, with that charter... I feel badly about that charter... You can't tell Mangini what happened. I hope they don't report it to Mangini."

"I doubt they will. It was an honest mistake."

"Even when you try to do right... And sometimes you can't even get up the courage to try to do right, but even when you try to do right, you..."

He was staring out the window now. His eyes were wide and glazed over, like he had just undergone some kind of hypnosis. Then there was a knock at the door. Mangini leaned his head into the room.

"Garrett, you're getting me those time sheets today, right?"

"Yep, Chief, on it. They're basically all done."

"Well finish 'em."

"Okay, Chief."

Mangini closed the door and Garrett began opening the drawers of his desk, looking for time sheets.

"Shit," Garrett said. "I gotta get this done. Why did you come in here? Did you need something?"

Berg explained how Woody had asked him if there were any jobs available at Fernwood.

"Woody?" Garrett asked. "Oh right, Woody, yeah, I know him. I dunno, sure."

"Sure?"

"You want less hours anyway, right? So you can abandon us for the boatbuilders. So yeah, sure."

"He says he's down to do whatever you need him to do."

"Yeah, okay. Let me check with Mangini. But it's probably all good."

Berg stood up to go and Garrett stopped rummaging through his drawers.

"By the way," he said. "That talk we just had that was between you and me."

"Okay, Garrett."

"Goes no further."

"You got it."

CHAPTER 16

WHEN MIMI RETURNED FROM Bali, Berg moved into the cubby on the lofting floor. The cubby was a triangle-shaped space that slanted downward with the slope of the barn's roof. It was exactly wide enough to fit a queen-size bed, a small lamp, and a few books. You had to crouch down to enter the cubby but once you were inside, it was relatively comfortable. Berg's main concern was the lack of ventilation, but there was a small, one-by-one window on the right that could be opened, and this proved sufficient. It didn't really matter anyway because he spent all of his time working in the shop.

The *Alma* was basically ready to go. The rig had been finished, the seams caulked, the bottom painted, the cabin top varnished, and the zincs prepared for sacrifice. In the few weeks before the launch, they equipped the boat with a self-steering system and GPS. Alejandro also finished installing a used propeller shaft, which he'd attached with a rubber pipe, two wooden washers cut from black locust, and several tightening bands. He often improvised systems like this to avoid purchasing new products from marine-supply stores.

"It keeps the cost of everything down," he explained.

Helping build the *Alma*, Berg had felt good for the first time in years. When he was working with wood he could get outside of himself, escape whatever it was that was dogging him. His mind no longer jumped from place to place, as it had when he first began sharpening chisels. It was quieter. It stayed in the room. It let him work peacefully, chisel and hammer in hand, light stealing through the tall shop windows.

"Enjoy every cut," Alejandro would say. "Why not enjoy every cut?"

Alejandro said he liked boatbuilding because it involved the self but it was not selfish. There was room for creativity, but the realities of the physical world also had to be accounted for. And there was little ambiguity in terms of execution. The joint either fit or it did not fit. The blade cut well enough or it needed to be sharpened more. Berg learned how to do things properly and, with each success, he felt more confident, more connected to the world. Alejandro observed this one day when Berg showed him a hollowing plane he'd made on his own out of a piece of pepperwood.

"See, it's nice to do things right," he said. "You do this one little thing right, in this moment, you fix this one little thing, and then you think, Maybe I can fix my life."

Alejandro had been an anthropologist before becoming a boatbuilder. He'd lived with Rebecca in Mexico and studied the matriarchal society structure of the Zapotec. He had also studied native cultures in Utah and Colorado. He never did any official anthropological work in California, but he was familiar with much of its indigenous history. He was particularly interested in the Chumash, who had built redwood canoes and sailed them to the Channel Islands. The redwood planks were sewn together and caulked with asphaltum, from the seeps in the Santa Barbara Channel.

"But the most spectacular thing," he said, "is that the Chumash had never seen a redwood. They got it all from the sea! It was driftwood. They understood it as a gift from the sea. The ocean had given them the wood so they could travel across it. Isn't that beautiful? I think that's just so damn beautiful."

Over time, Berg learned about Alejandro's father, about his childhood growing up on *Hoku Lewa*. He learned about Alejandro's first gale at sea, about hanging bags of stinking fish oil from the catheads, about the lightning and the burning, salty cold. And he learned about another gale in which Alejandro's father stayed up for thirty-six hours straight, guiding the schooner through every swell, yelling at him to heave coils of manila over the stern to slow the boat and prevent it from broaching.

On occasion, he told stories about apprentices who had worked in his shop or people in town. This was how Berg first learned about Pat the Pilot. Alejandro referred to him as JC's "vice president." He said he had known Pat for years and taught him how to sail and build. Pat coordinated JC's trimming operation, in those days, but in the offseason he'd work for Alejandro in the shop. Apparently Pat was the one who had introduced Alejandro and JC and laid the foundation for their business relationship. Over time, as JC's operation became more nautically focused, Pat rose up in the ranks. Nowadays he handled the majority of JC's deliveries. Most recently, he had been on a trip to and from Belize.

Berg met Pat for the first time that January, at the launch party for the *Alma*. He was a clean, fit man who seemed equally ready to head up an army or give a speech on the Senate floor. Uffa said that he had grown up in Albany, Texas but moved out to Talinas many years ago. Apparently, as a child, he'd flown crop dusters, which was where his nickname came from.

At the launch party there was cake and champagne and jugs of Rebecca's house wine. Alejandro's whole family was there, along with Uffa and Nell and, surprisingly, Garrett. Berg had told him about the event but he hadn't expected him to come. When he arrived he slapped Berg on the back.

"Check out this boat, homes," he said. "Hell yeah. Where's the booze?"

The vessel sat low in the water, like most of Alejandro's boats, with less than a foot of freeboard amidships. For its christening, Uffa smashed a watermelon over its bow. Alejandro hated the ritual of breaking a champagne bottle over the bow, so boats from their shop were always christened with watermelons. Afterwards, Uffa, Berg, and Alejandro hopped on the boat and Rebecca took a photo of them.

"Berg, smile," she said. "C'mon, give us that thousand-watt smile."

Once the photos had been taken, Alejandro introduced Berg and Pat. The three of them talked about the boat for a while, and then Alejandro asked Pat who was going to be the captain for the *Alma*'s inaugural trip to Mexico. Pat said that it would be him, and that they were leaving next week.

"Next week?" Alejandro said. "Why so soon?"

"That's what JC wants."

"Is it Michoacán?"

"Yes."

"Well, make sure you check for northers near Baja. You might get hit by the jet stream coming over from Hawaii, too."

"I'll keep an eye on it."

"Why is JC always in such a hurry?"

"I don't know," Pat said. "I just follow orders."

"It must be a big haul," Alejandro said. Pat didn't say anything. Just smiled and winked.

Also at the launch party was JC's girlfriend, Lammy. Uffa said he was surprised that she was here, that she rarely made public appearances. She had long black hair and smelled like tree oils. She spent most of the party over by the picnic table, speaking to Garrett. After she left, Garrett approached Berg and Uffa.

"What would you say if I told you I just met the woman of my dreams?" Garrett said.

"Forget about it, Garrett," Uffa said.

"Did Shakespeare tell Romeo to forget about Juliet?"

"Forget about it."

"But I'm in love."

"That's JC's girlfriend, Garrett. Are you out of your mind?"

Garrett looked sick.

"Strike that from the record," he said, and then he walked over to the picnic table to get a slice of cake.

CHAPTER 17

THE BEST PLACE TO see a boat leave Talinas was Bear's Landing. These days it was a campground but, according to Alejandro, it had first been settled by Ed Vaquero, an American who gathered abalone and whose last name was not actually Vaquero. No one knew his real name, Alejandro said, but it was not Vaquero. In any case, if you climbed up on the dunes behind the campground at Bear's Landing, you had a panoramic view of the bay and the ocean and this is what Uffa, Berg, and Alejandro did the day Pat left for Mexico.

It was a cold day, with the wind coming from the west, like

always, and Berg was wearing a jacket and a beanie. The three of them watched the *Alma* approach the mouth of the bay with some trepidation. The shoal by the mouth often produced breakers at the beginning of the ebb tide. Every year at least one fisherman died near the mouth, Alejandro said, usually caught unawares by a breaker. One year thirteen people died.

But Pat and his crew passed through the mouth with no problems. As Berg watched the boat head out into the vast cabbage-green sea, he thought about all the lives it would lead. For so long the boat had been sitting in Alejandro's shop, inanimate, but now it was out in the world, departing on its first adventure. He understood then what Alejandro had meant when he told Berg that he saw boats as living things. They had been in his study, late at night, looking at lines.

"You see all of these boats," he had said. "They have spirits. They are animals to me."

Berg felt connected to the *Alma*, invested in its future. He imagined, years later, running into the owner of the boat, whoever that was at the time, and learning about everything that had happened to it. He imagined crawling inside the cabin and looking around, seeing how everything had aged.

Later that night he lay in bed, in the cubby, with Nell. She had wanted to come up earlier in the day to see the boat depart, but she couldn't make it. She was working a shoot in the city that ran late. It was a fast-food commercial and they couldn't get the lighting right for the cheeseburger.

"I'm not even kidding," she said. "They were fixing the lighting on this cheeseburger for like four hours."

Nell was absentmindedly flipping through one of the Persian poetry books in the cubby. Alejandro had lots of different books in the main house—ethnographies and novels and histories, books on architecture and sailing and keeping bees—but up in the cubby, for some reason, there was only Persian poetry. All of the books were inscribed in the top right corner with Alejandro's initials, A. V.

"Does Alejandro ever take the boats down to Mexico?" Nell asked.

"No, he just builds them."

"Why do they need so many of them?"

"I think the business keeps expanding. And also they don't want to keep sending the same boats down there. It would look suspicious."

"Do you know what kind of drugs they traffic?"

"Just weed."

"No opioids?"

"No opioids," Berg said.

Nell laughed. "This is a sketchy little scene you've gotten yourself wound up in," she said.

"Nah, it's not that sketchy."

She flipped a page in the book she was looking at.

"These poems are pretty good," she said. "Is Alejandro Persian?"

"I don't think so," Berg said.

"Do you think his children know how strange their life is?"

"I feel like the older ones do. I don't know about Tess."

"She reminds me of myself as a kid," Nell said. "Just this floating orb of energy, drifting from one imaginary narrative to the next." She paused for a second. "I didn't even know what I was at that age, didn't have a sense of myself as possessing a body. It was so liberating. You could become anything. I remember this one week, when this huge imaginary playground battle took place. I was in kindergarten, probably about Tess's age, and a feud developed between Ellen Wilson and Danny Sartori. It had to do with something insane, like him thinking she cut him in line for the slide. But everybody took sides, and it became this vast rooftop playground battle. Our playground was on a rooftop. We were city kids.

"For that whole week, Ellen Wilson was this queen, commanding her army. At the beginning of every break, the respective armies would line up at either end of the playground, and then they'd rush each other. Combat consisted of tagging another person. If you got tagged then you were taken to the opposing army's jail. You could be rescued from jail if someone from your army was able to run up and tag your hand without first getting tagged by one of the other army's jail guards. We were riffing on Capture the Flag but it was also something else. Ellen had jesters and courtesans who surrounded her while she sat on her throne, which was two milk crates stacked on top of each other. I was one of the jesters. I told stories and sang songs for the court. I invented this whole mythology about our people and their culture. I was so nerdy. Pathologically nerdy. Also, I was obsessed with Ellen Wilson. She was the coolest and I was always trying to impress her.

"I remember the yard monitors were so perplexed by the whole thing. They had none of the background story, had no idea why we were doing this or how the dynamics of this game had been so quickly and widely disseminated. But for us, playing was so intuitive. We found a common thread and *boom*, we were off to the races. That's what Tess is like right now. It's beautiful. I hope she gets to keep that for as long as possible."

She closed the poetry book and put it back on the shelf. Then she scanned the spines to find something new.

"Nell?" Berg said.

"Yeah?" she said, craning her neck to look at him.

"I love you."

CHAPTER 18

AFTER THE LAUNCH OF the *Alma*, they began work on a new sloop for JC. This boat would be for his own personal use on the bay. It was the vessel Alejandro had been designing on the loft floor the first day Berg met him, and it was going to be a thirty-four-foot sloop, with a fairly large rig to counteract the size of its beam and draft, which were both greater than average. Alejandro had based the design on the old American centerboard sloops, which the French had become enamored with and adapted to create their Clipper ships. Alejandro loved pointing out that it was these boats that had captured the imagination of Impressionist painters like Monet, Renoir, and Manet, who featured them in their paintings of the races at Argenteuil. When Nell had visited the week before, he explained the origin of these sloops, and he and Nell bonded over their mutual love of Caillebotte.

Before they could begin building JC's sloop, however, they needed to mill more wood. Alejandro milled all of the wood he used to build boats with an Alaskan chainsaw mill. His old boat-building mentor, Orhan, had designed the mill, which featured a simple handle that was attached to the chainsaw with two long cords. Using a choke-style throttle, Alejandro ran the mill at a high rpm to prevent the chainsaw from stalling mid-cut. It wasn't as clean or accurate as the machinery used at a proper sawmill, but it was portable, and it allowed them to harvest trees along any roadside in the county.

The most important part of milling wood, Alejandro explained, was finding the right tree. Often, they were able to scavenge wood, to mill a tree that had already fallen on some rancher's property. But regardless of whether they cut down the tree themselves or scavenged it, it was crucial to select the perfect tree, because milling took several days, and if you chose poorly, it could end up being a huge waste of time.

"We're like sushi chefs," Alejandro said. "We need the finest materials. The tree really has to be just right."

The first time Berg went scouting for wood with Alejandro, they drove up into the hills behind Talinas. Alejandro parked the car in a turnout on Kehoe Road and they walked along Bass Creek. He pointed out different species of plant as they hiked next to the creek. White alder, big-leaf maple, ferns, coffeeberry shrub.

Al Garther owned all of this land, Alejandro said, and he let them mill on it. Al had made his money in some sort of

Asian-clothing-marketing concern that Alejandro chose not to ask too many questions about. Al lived in a house at the northernmost end of the property and rented the house on the southwest corner of the property to Leanne Korver, the local Pilates teacher and the mother of Demeter, the woman Uffa had begun seeing. Berg hadn't spent that much time hanging out with Demeter but Uffa was clearly smitten.

"She's a mystic alpha queen born under a wolf moon," he'd told Berg the other day.

Alejandro hobbled along the banks of the creek and Berg followed after him. On occasion Alejandro paused to study the bark of a pepperwood tree. He needed one that grew straight up, he said, and had no wind twist and few branches. These types of trees were usually found on the northern slopes of hills, where trees had to grow very quickly in order to reach the sun and, as a result, could not waste energy creating limbs. Trees like this produced straight wood that flexed the proper amount and had few knots.

Berg found one good pepperwood tree but it was not close enough to the road for the wood to be milled and then feasibly transported. Around midday they stopped and ate lunch: chicken salad sandwiches and pickles and molasses cookies. They drank green tea from a thermos and dangled their feet in the creek. It was cold but not too cold, like a glass of ice water left out on the counter for an hour.

Alejandro had milled several trees along this creek and it was always one of the first places he visited on a scouting expedition. The pepperwood from around here tended to be extra resistant to rot for reasons he couldn't completely explain. When he'd first started milling, he'd performed all sorts of tests on the wood in the region. He would bury planks from different trees in the forest and then come back to examine the extent of their decay. White oak, black oak, Douglas fir, pepperwood, black locust, eucalyptus. He dropped sledgehammers on them from various heights. He soaked them in water. He had cataloged all of this work and self-published a small pamphlet called *A Study of the Trees in Talinas: With a Focus on Milling, With a Special Focus on Milling for Boatbuilding*. He had shown Berg a copy of the pamphlet at his house. Alejandro is many things, Berg remembered thinking, but he is not great with titles.

Berg wiped his feet dry with the sleeve of his shirt and put his boots back on. Alejandro walked several yards away from the creek, barefoot, and peed on a patch of poison oak. Then they continued to follow the creek. Every once in a while Alejandro stopped, knelt down to examine a plant or an animal track. He took clippings of Mexican tea and dandelion greens, stuffed them in his backpack.

At a certain point, the road peeled away from the creek and Berg and Alejandro followed it. As they moved away from the creek, the flora began to shift: now there was tanbark oak and madrone, a few redwoods. To their left a meadow unfolded, the grass soft and smooth like a green tablecloth stretched over the ground.

While they searched, Alejandro talked about why he thought it was important to mill their own wood. It was cheaper, for one thing, and better for the environment. But also, it made them reliant on the world around them. Alejandro was very critical of sophistication. He believed that confusion and trouble grew out of complexity. He wanted people to have an intimate relationship with their own environment. The problem, he said, was that people had become too dissociated from the circumstances and conditions of their immediate surroundings. They treated the land around them with indifference and inattention, because they did not feel like they relied on it in any substantive way.

"Many people have written about this," he said. "But it continues to be true. We continue to live, by and large, apart from the land. If you work the land, you begin to understand how much you need it, how much it underpins your entire existence. And also," he said, stopping by the creek and pulling out his water bottle, "you develop an affection for it. When we really pay attention to a thing, we begin to love it, and then we care for it."

It was Berg who found the tree, hours later: a majestic pepperwood with small green leaves and very few branches. No wind twist whatsoever, if the appearance of the bark could be trusted. They took the leaves and crushed them in their hands, inhaled the sharp medicinal smell. Pepperwoods were also known as headache trees, Alejandro explained, because their scent was thought to both provoke and cure headaches, depending on who sniffed them.

"This is the one," Alejandro said, pleased but exhausted. "This is a beautiful tree, Berg. This is a beautiful tree."

Alejandro tied a piece of red cloth around one of the branches so they could see it from the road. Then he hobbled over to a nearby rock and sat down gingerly. He looked to be in some degree of discomfort.

"Are you okay, Ale?" Berg asked.

"Yes, my hip's been sore lately. I went to the doctor to check it out and he told me it might get better if we just let it alone, but man, it's killing me right now."

Berg thought about the fact that Alejandro would die someday. Perhaps soon. Who could say? So much would be lost when it happened. Berg could barely bring himself to consider it. It was too sad.

He set down his pack and joined Alejandro on the rock.

"Can I do anything for you?" he said.

"No, it's fine. I just need to rest a moment."

They sat quietly, listened to the sounds of the forest. Alejandro took out a piece of smoked trout from his backpack and broke off half of it for Berg, as if it were a chocolate bar.

"You know, Berg," he said. "Nell told me about your concussion. I was very sorry to hear about that."

"What did she tell you about it?"

"The whole thing: the concussion, the pain pills, rehab."

Berg took a bite of the trout. He felt blindsided, betrayed. Why had Nell told Alejandro about all that? This had always been the problem in their relationship. Nell thought it was better to reveal everything and Berg preferred that some things remain undisclosed. Why didn't she consider that the story of his suffering and his addiction was his to tell?

"If you ever want to talk about it, I am here," Alejandro continued.

"Thanks," Berg said. "I don't need to talk, but thanks."

"Okay."

"I'm sorry. I'd just... I'd rather not talk about it."

"That's fine, Berg," he said. "Let's go home."

They finished eating the trout and wiped the grease off on their pants. Before they left, Alejandro admired the pepperwood one more time.

"Yes," he said, seeming satisfied. "Time to go home."

CHAPTER 19

"I DIDN'T KNOW YOU hadn't told them," Nell said on the phone that night. "I'm sorry. You're right, it's your story to tell, but I just assumed you had told them. I mean, you've been living and working with these people all day every day for what? The last six months?"

"Well, you should have asked me first," Berg said.

"Okay, you're right," she said. "I'm sorry. I apologize for that."

Berg looked out the window of the cubby. The trees behind the farmhouse looked green and bunchy, like broccoli florets.

"I still want you to come up this weekend," Berg said, his voice softening.

"I was still planning on it," she said. "Can I ask you a question?"

"Yes."

"Why didn't you tell them? Why don't you talk about it?"

"I don't know," Berg said.

"You didn't do anything wrong, Berg. You had a concussion. You kept having all those headaches. They prescribed you painkillers."

"I know."

"So there's nothing to be ashamed about, right?" Nell said.

"Right."

After they hung up he leaned back in bed. The things Nell said were not untrue, but they were incomplete. The way she told it, he was blameless. But he didn't feel like that. He felt responsible. He needed to be responsible. If he wasn't, then he lost all agency, any ability to combat the problem.

He thought back to beginning of everything, to the concussion, three years ago. It had been a long time since he'd been skiing and he was having a nice time. Nell was down at the lodge and he was out on the slopes by himself. The air smelled like pine and hard rock and sweet alpine meadow. The sounds of the mountain were muted and seemed to come one at a time, emerging in their full particularity and then disappearing back into the white silence: the flap of a bird's wing, the scrape of a snowboarder passing him on his right, carving her way through the ice.

When Berg had finished the first few blue squares he felt ready for something more difficult. He took a lift to the top of the mountain, which would allow him to take any number of routes back to the bottom. Once up there, he approached a man who was wearing a red shirt that said STAFF. The man's face looked red and burned, like a piece of meat that had just been taken out of the freezer. Berg asked him what the easiest black diamond was and the man said, "Devil's Gulch."

Devil's Gulch was not the easiest black diamond. Berg would learn this an hour later, as he sat in the emergency first-aid hut at the bottom of the mountain, getting examined by a nurse with a shaved head.

"What run were you coming down?" the nurse asked.

"Devil's Gulch."

"Oh boy," the nurse had said.

But Berg had no time to be angry. Or, rather, he didn't have the capacity to be angry. He could not think. His head felt like a wide-open field. The field was full of crickets and Tylenol pills and the occasional question from Nell, who drove him to the hospital, where they took an X-ray of his brain to make sure that he wasn't bleeding internally and then sent him home with a pamphlet about concussions and his first ever bottle of hydrocodone. He sat down on the hotel couch and closed his eyes. He felt off balance and a little queasy and there was often a humming in his ears. At times he felt immensely peaceful and other times he felt afraid and angry. He saw various shapes and overall, he told Nell, it felt a little bit like he was on mushrooms. After the hydrocodone kicked in, he fell asleep on the couch, and then Nell helped him move into bed. In the middle of the night he woke up, terrified that someone was going to break into the house. He lay awake, convinced that it was only a matter of time before someone busted through the door and attacked him and his girlfriend. Eventually he fell back asleep. In the morning, when he woke up, he remembered only certain moments from the previous day. He remembered hitting the mogul and flying face first into the sheet of ice. He remembered someone calling out to him from a chairlift overhead, asking if he was okay. He remembered talking to the nurse at the bottom of the hill. He did not remember getting an X-ray. He did not remember fearing a break-in at midnight.

Nell drove him home the following day. It was a bright day, with a bright sky and a few clouds, very high up, that seemed to have no interest in getting any closer to earth. Berg and Nell listened to a book on tape and blasted the heat and stopped, at one point, to eat cheeseburgers and pie.

"How do you feel?" Nell asked him.

"Better," he had said. "I feel better already."

CHAPTER 20

BY MARCH, THEY'D MADE good progress on JC's sloop. The stem and stern were cut, the frames were up, and the lead keel had been cast. It was around this time that someone stole Alejandro's van and dumped it in the ravine by the 12. They never figured out who did it but, at some point, Freddie Moltisanti told Uffa that he thought it was a group of teenagers who had taken it. Freddie never said how he knew this, and Alejandro didn't believe him. Freddie was prone to lying. When he was younger, Freddie had been something of a local celebrity because he ran away from home for a week and lived in a cave. He was twelve years old and, allegedly, he survived on wild apples and several packages of saltines. Alejandro didn't believe this story either.

In any case, the car was totaled and irretrievable and Alejandro left it in the ravine. A few weeks after it was stolen, JC stopped by the shop. Berg could tell he was important the moment he walked in. People often came by to see Alejandro. Joe Leggett was right that certain people thought Alejandro was crazy, but others clearly respected him. Neighbors would stop in with an extra fish they'd caught or some fresh corn or a root that they were trying to identify. They came around lunchtime and waited patiently outside the barn until Alejandro had finished his work. But JC didn't do this. He stormed into the barn early one morning with no advance notice. He was a large man, two hundred pounds or so of sauntering muscle, and he wore a red knitted beanie. A smoky, fruity odor clung to him, as if he'd just come from a hookah bar.

"Alejandro!" he shouted. "You guys are doing great things. I need you to come with me for a second. I'm gonna show you something."

To Berg's surprise, Alejandro agreed. He had never seen Alejandro put down his work in the middle of the day for some random request. In fact, the most predictable way to irritate Alejandro was to distract him from his work. Now that Berg had done some boatbuilding, he understood why. The work required serious focus and any diversion made it that much more difficult.

As Alejandro and JC walked out of the shop, JC noticed Berg.

"Hey, who are you?" he asked.

Berg looked up from the plank he was spiling and introduced himself.

"This a new guy?" JC said to Alejandro. "You didn't tell me that you had a new guy."

"Berg's been with us for several months now," Alejandro said.

"Fuck yeah!" JC shouted. "Berg! My man. You're coming with us, too. Come on."

Berg looked at Alejandro and Alejandro smiled. "Come on," he said. "You can finish that later."

Alejandro and Berg got into JC's Mercedes and they drove into the hills behind Talinas. Berg sat in the front seat and Alejandro sat in the back.

"I love that new boat you guys built, man," JC said. "The *Alma*. I love it. It's perfect. With the compartments down below. It's great. What are those made out of again?"

"Iroko," Alejandro said. "It's the most durable hardwood we have."

"Amazing. I love it," JC said.

He opened the glove box and pulled out a pack of beef jerky, offered some to Alejandro and Berg. There was a gun in the glove compartment. Berg took the beef jerky and chewed it slowly, looked out the window at the bay as it receded from view.

"I heard about your car," JC said to Alejandro, taking a big bite of the jerky and chewing it loudly. "Some motherfuckers stole your car."

"Yes," Alejandro said.

"Motherfuckers," JC scowled.

After several minutes they rounded a corner and began heading up JC's driveway. When they got to the top of the driveway, Berg saw Lammy and her kids. They were playing soccer in a grassy field, and behind them, in the distance, Berg could see a house. The house was built in the shape of a mushroom, or perhaps a snail? It was hard to say. Lammy came over and kissed Alejandro on the cheek.

"It's so good to see you," she said.

"It's good to see you, dear," Alejandro said.

"You showing him his present?" Lammy asked.

"Yep," JC said.

"You're gonna like it," Lammy said, and then she called to the kids and retreated toward the house.

JC winked at Berg and then ushered them over to his garage. He lifted up the door to reveal several motorcycles and a brand new Cadillac. JC motioned toward the Cadillac like a game-show host.

"I bought you a Cadillac," JC said, grinning at Alejandro. Alejandro stood there silently, staring at the Cadillac. JC motioned to the Cadillac again: "It's yours," he said. "Happy birthday. It's a birthday present. You can take Rebecca out on a drive."

"But it's not my birthday," Alejandro said.

"It's for your last birthday then, whatever."

"JC…" Alejandro began.

"You don't want it," JC said. "I can tell. You don't want it. That's totally fine, man. Totally fine."

Berg looked at JC fearfully. He had no idea if he was being serious.

"Just do me a favor," JC said. "Just drive it down to the water. You and Berg. Follow me down to the water in the Cadillac. I'm going to take the Mercedes. Just follow me down. You don't have to accept the gift."

He handed Alejandro the keys, hopped into his Mercedes, and cruised down the driveway. Berg's first thought was, of course, that JC was going to murder them and dump them in the bay. He thought of the gun in the glove compartment. His mouth was dry and tasted like beef jerky.

Alejandro said nothing as they drove down the hill but, Berg noticed, his knuckles were white from gripping the wheel.

"How bad is this?" Berg asked.

"It's not good," Alejandro said.

"You should have just accepted the Cadillac."

"I hate Cadillacs."

"Jesus. Are we about to get fucked up?"

"I hope not."

They parked on the turnout by Miller's Point, about fifteen yards away from the cliff. JC got out of the car and walked over to the Cadillac.

"Okay, put the thing in neutral," he said.

"Look, JC," Alejandro said, still sitting in the car, the door open. "Let me explain…"

"No, man! You don't want it! No need to explain. Put the thing in neutral and get out."

Alejandro put it in neutral and he and Berg exited the car. Then JC asked them to help him push it.

"Push it off the cliff?" Berg said.

"Off the edge, man! Off the edge!"

It was difficult to get the car rolling but JC was an absurdly strong man. With his help, they were able to get it moving and, once it picked up speed, they gave it one last shove and stepped back. Alejandro bent over and panted like a linebacker, but JC walked to the edge of the cliff and watched the Cadillac plummet to the rocks below. It must have been a fifty-foot drop.

"Fuck yeah!" JC yelled and scrambled down a path on the side of the cliff toward the car. Once he was down on the beach, he began picking up rocks and throwing them at the car, smashing its windows, denting the parts of it that were not yet dented from its fall.

"Fuck this Cadillac, man! Fuck it!" he yelled. Berg watched him from the top of the cliff, still slightly terrified, but also relieved. Several minutes later JC scrambled back up the cliff and shook Alejandro's hand. He was covered in sweat, but he seemed relaxed, like he'd just had a massage.

"Okay, man," he said. "I'll drop you guys home now. Happy birthday, Ale."

CHAPTER 21

ONE SUNDAY, ALEJANDRO OFFERED to take Berg and Uffa out on
one of the four boats he kept down by the dock. In the morning
they drank coffee and ate rye bread with butter and then they
headed down to the water. Alejandro's dock was shaped like a *T*
and it extended probably thirty feet out into the bay. There were
two boats tied up along the body of the *T*, and two boats further
out, tied to the top of the *T*. On shore, flipped upside down, were
several canoes.

"See, this boat here," Alejandro said, walking over to one of
the canoes. "This boat is so light. I built this boat so you could

carry it by yourself. See?" He lifted the boat and winced slightly. "It's perfect," he said, still wincing, "for going to get your groceries in the morning. When I lived at Dillon Beach, I used to row this down to Five Brooks when I needed provisions. And this one," he said pointing to a larger boat, "this is the one we're taking out: *Contos*."

The *Contos* was based on the Greek salmon boats that used to be sailed near Vallejo. She was sprit-rigged and beamy, but still fast and maneuverable. She was capable of carrying over two thousand five hundred pounds of fish and designed to be sailed underweight. The boat had a small cabin and she was equipped with a dory, which fit neatly on her foredeck.

Uffa uncleated the dock lines and shoved the boat off the pier, hopping onto the stern at the last moment. Alejandro's house was located on the eastern shore of the bay and his pier edged out into a shallow cove. The cove was pretty much clear of obstacles, except for one rock near its center, which was submerged during high tide but visible during low tide, covered with slippery green seaweed. Alejandro had strung two leading lights from madrone trees near the shore so he could navigate past the rock if he had to return after dark.

They tacked their way up to the mouth and crossed the shoal with little difficulty. Once out of the bay, the winds picked up and shifted slightly to the north. To the west they could see the Slide Islands, rocky and brown, and to the east the coastal ridge, with its white, wave-cut bluffs. They sailed south now on a broad reach, less than a mile from the shore. Berg managed the jib, trimming the sheet every once in while to keep the sail full. When they passed the lighthouse they jibed and headed east, toward Wildcat Bay and Estero. This was the bay where the first English explorers had landed in the sixteenth century, looking for treasure. According to Alejandro, they had described the cliffs as reminiscent of the English Channel.

"When I first came here with my father," Alejandro said, "I thought California was so ugly. I thought it was gray and cold and ugly. I was coming from Tahiti, you know, where everything is very bright and tropical. It wasn't until I had lived in Talinas for several years that I began to appreciate the beauty here. It's similar to what we were talking about the other day, Berg," he said. "It takes time to build affection for something. You have to stay in a place. It doesn't just happen instantly."

Once inside the bay, all three of them squeezed into the dory and rowed to shore. They pulled the dory up onto the beach, its bottom scraping against the sand, and then they began to hike east into the estuary. Winter was still holding on, it seemed, and the sky was moon-white and pockmarked. Along the shore delicate herons stood knee-deep in the water and, in the distance, rows of oyster racks lay exposed in the low tide. Berg knew there was some kind of controversy about the oyster farm in Estero but he hadn't paid close attention to it.

While they were walking, Uffa mentioned that he was thinking about going back to school.

"For what?" Alejandro asked, skeptically.

"MFA," he said. "Get an MFA in poetry."

Alejandro took a blue bandanna from his pocket and wiped his nose.

"You don't approve," Uffa said, watching him. "I know."

"Do you want to be a poet?" Alejandro asked, shoving the bandanna back into his pocket.

"I like writing poetry," Uffa said.

"But where does it lead you?" Alejandro said. "I don't see

the value. The best that can happen is that you create a cult of personality."

"Are you kidding?" Uffa said. "I totally disagree. It's art. Art is important. You practice an art yourself."

"Yes, but it has a practical application."

"Delivering drugs?"

"I've been building boats for years, Uffa, and the boats have been used for all different sorts of things: fishing, traveling…"

"I know, but I mean, c'mon, Ale. Poetry is exciting. It's beautiful."

"I know it's exciting. I've no doubt it's exciting," Alejandro said. "But it's a dead end."

The two of them continued to argue in this fashion for the next several minutes. Alejandro saw poetry and writing as leading to madness. It could only be made on luxury time, he argued, could only be created out of profound boredom. To Alejandro's mind, poetry distracted from the real work that needed to be done. As an artist, in the best-case scenario, all you did was cultivate your persona. You were left with nothing except an image of yourself as the poet and then you were dead.

"I would rather be in the world," Alejandro said. "That is what I find beautiful. I'll take the life of the peasant. Poetry is just empty sophistication. And sophistication is how we got into this whole mess in the first place."

"I think it's useful," Uffa said.

"It leads toward madness in the end, Uffa."

"That's what happened to Szerbiak. That's not what's going to happen to me."

"I never said anything about Szerbiak."

"I know you didn't."

Berg had never heard Alejandro articulate his positions on

poetry but he was not surprised by them. Alejandro held extreme views about many things. He believed the American empire was crumbling, and in a sense, he had moved his family to the country to build his ark and raise his children by the bay. Still, there was something hard in his voice when he argued with Utta about poetry, something defensive and pained. Berg had the sense that he only half-believed the things he was saying, which was rare for Alejandro, who usually spoke with conviction. For a moment, Berg began to doubt Alejandro, to doubt his entire reality. Was he just some bitter old hermit? Or was he worth listening to, worth looking up to? The arguments he was making were logical, but they seemed cruel.

Berg had seen pictures of Alejandro with the young Szerbiak. This was when the two of them were both living in Colorado, fresh out of college. Alejandro was working as an anthropologist and Szerbiak was working on his first novel. There was a copy of that book on Alejandro's bookshelf. Szerbiak had signed it and written a long inscription. Berg didn't know what had happened between the two of them. He knew that Szerbiak had died a long time ago, after years of drinking.

When Berg first began to get to know Alejandro, he had the sense that Alejandro and his family had existed in this fashion for all of time. There was something eternal about them. Their life had such a clear rhythm, such steady purpose. It was hard to imagine them being anything other than the people he'd encountered when he first arrived. And yet, clearly, they had forged this world from something altogether different. They had inhabited different existences in different times. All you had to do was look at that picture of Alejandro and Szerbiak, the two of them dressed in sharp black suits, to know that, for Alejandro, many other lives had preceded this one.

CHAPTER 22

THE WESTERN WAS LOCATED on the bay, next door to Gary's Oysters and Vlasic's Boat Works. Before settling into its present capacity as a bar, it had served, at different times, as a dry goods store, a horse stable, a brothel, a temporary jail, and a flophouse. It had swinging doors and a fireplace and pool tables that cost seventy-five cents a game. Uffa liked to go there because they served a chi chi, which was the only alcoholic beverage he ever drank, a sweet rum cocktail that tasted like ice cream.

Uffa usually drank his chi chi within two minutes but today he was slipping it slowly. Berg was drinking a beer. To their right a woman was talking about the great deal she got at an outlet store: 50 percent off, when all was said and done. She'd had many coupons. Berg didn't know anyone here. The Western and the Tavern seemed to have entirely different clientele, even though they were owned and run by the same family. In front of them, on the screen above the bar, there was a college football game. Mississippi was upsetting LSU. The LSU quarterback kept shaking his head, squirting himself in the face with his water bottle.

"You know," Uffa said. "I first came to Talinas because I had read about Alejandro in Szerbiak's books."

"He's in Szerbiak's books? Which ones?"

"The first two. I mean, he doesn't feature prominently, but he's in there. He's the anthropologist they meet up with in Mexico."

"Oh yeah, I think I remember him. I've only ever read the second one."

"In one interview Szerbiak acknowledges that the character is based on Alejandro," Uffa said. "Most of his characters were based on real people. And in that same interview, Szerbiak describes Alejandro as the most brilliant person he ever met."

"Damn," Berg said, impressed.

"Does that surprise you?"

"I guess not."

"Doesn't surprise me," Uffa said. "Anyway, I had read about Alejandro in Szerbiak's books and in that interview and I heard he was in Talinas and, you know, I was a sixteen-year-old journeyman-poet-loose-cannon… I thought I'd go pay him a visit. He ended up taking me in, teaching me how to build boats. This was back when he was still working with his old partner at Dillon Beach. Before he moved across the bay to this newer property."

Behind them the swinging doors creaked. You always knew

when someone was entering the Western because of its noisy doors. Berg and Uffa glanced over their shoulders to see who had arrived. It was a young ranch hand that neither of them recognized.

"I didn't know it then," Ulla continued, "but Alejandro and Szerbiak had fallen out of friendship years before Szerbiak's death. Mostly because Alejandro was tired of taking part in Szerbiak's bohemian shenanigans. He wanted to have a family and land and Szerbiak wanted to keep taking drugs and drinking and driving around in cars."

"It's hard to imagine Ale as a hedonistic young man, doing drugs in cars," Berg said.

"But that's what they did. And eventually, Ale got tired of it. I've heard him go off on that tangent about poetry being a dead end. I think it's just fear. You know, he once told me that he'd never be able to write every day. 'I'd never be able to do that, Uffa,' he said. 'I'd die.' And I believe him. I think he's terrified of it. I think he believes it destroyed his friend and I think it terrifies him. And then I have to stand there and listen to him shred poetry to pieces from some ideological high horse as though the two things are not remotely related."

Uffa took a sip of his chi chi.

"Sometimes Alejandro can be so stubborn," he said. "Especially when he gets into one of his states. You haven't seen that before. He gets obsessed with a thing and then he just spirals downward."

"I remember when he was into those lutes," Berg said.

"Yeah, that was a minor version of what I'm talking about. He kept that under control. What I'm talking about is when he really loses it. I've gotten calls from Rebecca twice where she asked me to drive up from Oakland to speak to him, calm him down. He gets trapped in his own mind, can't stop agonizing over things. You heard about the pigeons, right?"

The whole episode started, Uffa explained, when Alejandro saw a pigeon tumble from the sky to escape a hawk. This was not an uncommon thing for pigeons to do, to fake a fall to escape a hawk and then continue flying. But this bird did not continue flying. It fell and crashed into the earth. The same thing happened a month later and then again a few weeks after that. Alejandro read everything he could about tumbler pigeons but he was unable to find anything that accurately explained this phenomenon. So he began to breed pigeons himself, to try to figure out what made some of them skilled tumblers and what made others fall to their death. He built over ten cages, bred hundreds of pigeons.

"By the time I got up here," Uffa said, "he looked terrible. He hadn't been eating well. He smelled bad. Like a pigeon, honestly. He smelled like a pigeon."

"What did you do?" Berg asked.

"I just talked to him about the pigeons. I listened. That's the only thing you can do."

On the television, the game had ended. The Mississippi quarterback was giving a post-game interview, stating obvious things. Berg was almost done with his beer.

"So are you going to start the MFA next fall?" he asked.

"Oh, no, not that soon," Uffa said. "Can't afford it. That was more like a five-year plan. I was just throwing it out there."

CHAPTER 23

DEMETER WORE LARGE SWEATSHIRTS and tights. Her teeth were ragged and serrated, but this somehow only added to her fierce beauty. She'd moved to Talinas with her mother in high school and the two of them now ran a Pilates studio in town. Recently, it had been revealed that Demeter's mother disapproved of her relationship with Uffa, whom she saw as a bad influence.

"I know the type," she had reportedly told Demeter. "Rolls into town with a school bus and lots of talk about free expression."

But Leanne's indictment of Uffa did not seem to deter Demeter. Berg saw her around the bus more and more. She said she was saving up money to move to New York City and become an actor. Earlier that year she'd had a role in a Talinas Community College student film, which Uffa had screened on the bus with a projector. It was not good. This was not Demeter's fault. The finest of actors could not have rescued the script, which was about a young man who was upset that his girlfriend didn't take his band seriously enough. Uffa was particularly frustrated by the main male character.

"If he wants someone to care about his band," Uffa had said, "he's just gotta be his special regular self. He's all up in his head, man. No time for that."

One Saturday evening found Demeter, Berg, and Uffa hanging out on the bus, about to head down to the farmhouse for dinner. Demeter was sitting at the desk, drawing something Berg couldn't see. Uffa was taking shirts out of his milk crates and smelling them, trying to find a clean one.

Uffa wanted to have another bus show but he was tired of hosting them at Alejandro's house. The two of them were on better terms since their argument that day on Estero, but Berg could tell that Uffa didn't feel like asking Alejandro for any favors.

"How do we get into the Oysters stadium?" Uffa asked, pulling another shirt out of his milk crate. "That's what I really want to do. Have a show in the stadium."

"You'd have to ask Walt Weir," Demeter said, without looking up. "He's the basketball coach, but he also manages events at the stadium. He was coaching the girls team when I was in high school but now he coaches the boys."

"Coach man," Uffa said. "Okay, we can do that."

"I played on his team for a year in high school," Demeter said. "He's a cool guy. You'll like him. He's kind of a legend around here. He was an amazing athlete in his time and people still revere him. Tell him you know me." Demeter set down her pencil. "I gotta go," she said. She stood up and kissed Uffa on the cheek.

"You're not coming to dinner?" he asked.

"Nah, mom wants to have dinner," she called as she stepped off the bus.

After she was gone, Uffa turned to Berg.

"Gotta keep Mama Shark fed," he said.

Berg and Uffa drove over to the high school the following day to see Walt. They listened to the radio as they drove. Morty Weisenstein was on the air. His show featured ambient music, calypso, and Afro-Cuban music, and he was always shifting in and out of different DJ personas. Today, for example, he was hosting the show as the rabbi and musicologist Dr. Baruch Baruch, and he was making the argument that calypso had Hebraic roots.

"There is a similar lyric about bananas in the Mishnah," he said. "Although obviously it does not reference bananas. They had no bananas in Jerusalem, lamentably. But the connection goes very deep, you see. It's very profound and it has international implications."

Inside the gym, Walt Weir was pacing up and down the sidelines, wearing a tie-dye shirt and green sweatpants. Berg thought he looked a little bit like an older Uffa, but he didn't say that. The gym smelled like sweaty polyester and old wood and rubber. Berg and Uffa took a seat on the bleachers and watched the scrimmage. One of the bigger players drove to the hoop from the right side and was fouled as he went for a layup.

"Take it strong, Jaylen," Walt said. "Throw it down, big man. Throw it down once for me."

"I can't dunk, coach," Jaylen said as he was running back on defense.

"Then finish strong and fluid, Jaylen," Walt called after him. "Stay loose. This is basketball. This is poetry. This is a dance. You should be dancing up and down the floor."

Jaylen nodded and picked up his man on defense. The other team set a series of off-ball screens and then their point guard drove to the hoop. He attacked the right side and attempted a floater but Jaylen had cycled over to help and swatted the shot out of bounds.

"Yes, Jaylen!" Walt shouted. "That is leadership. That is courage. That is basketball. That is poetry. This is what I am talking about."

When the scrimmage was over Walt gathered the players together and ran over the coming week's schedule. They would have strength and conditioning every day and another open gym that Sunday.

"We are improving," Walt said. "We're getting better every day, but we've got to play with confidence. 'He who hesitates is lost.' Who said that? That was Pete Harrison, one of the greatest basketball coaches in the history of California. Perhaps one of the greatest coaches in the history of Western civilization. I had the privilege of going to his big man camp when I was younger. A wonderful, wonderful man. You know what else he said? 'Balance is the building block of good basketball.' We've got to stay grounded, we've got to stay composed. Run our offense, get our looks. The shots will drop. That's straight out of the mouth of the great Pete Harrison. Being with Pete on the court was like walking through Yosemite with John Muir, like traveling the Missouri River with Sacagawea, like hanging out on the beach with Eddie Aikau. Are you picking up what I'm putting down? Okay, bring it in. 'Seals' on three. One, two, three: Seals! See you tomorrow."

The team dispersed throughout the gym, looking a little dazed. Uffa and Berg stood up from the bleachers and headed over to Walt. They said hello and introduced themselves as Demeter's friends.

"Demeter!" he said. "An angel. An angel of mercy."

"How's it going?"

"I'm wonderful. What did you say your name was? Uffa? What an interesting name. Things are wonderful, Uffa. Nothing I'd rather be doing. I'm coaching basketball. I'm healthy. I can think. I can write. I can move. I can ride my bike. I can dream. I've got it all."

"You guys have a good team this year?"

"We've got some players. We've got some players. They need to get hip to certain fundamental things, but the passion is there. The creativity is there. The celebration, the dance, the vision. These things are there and growing stronger every day." Walt grinned. "Anyway, what can I do for you?" he said.

"We were wondering if you could help us book the Oysters stadium for a concert," Uffa said.

"A concert? Oh man, it's been so long since we've had a good show around here. We used to have great music here all the time. Gosh, I'd love to have a show over there. You want to do it on a weekend?"

"Yes."

"On a weekend the fee would be five hundred dollars for the entire day."

"Is there anyway you could bump that down?" Berg asked. "We both work as boatbuilders and we're very poor."

"With Alejandro?"

"Yes."

"Ale! What a man. A good great man. Tell him I say hello. I'll look into knocking down the price. You know, it's a concert, and we need concerts here, and now I know that you guys are with Ale... I'll look into it. I'll definitely look into it."

"Thanks, Walt."

They exited the gym through the swinging doors and Walt knelt down to unlock his yellow bicycle. "You guys coming to the Dance Palace banquet next week?" he asked. "They're honoring the Sharkman."

"Not sure yet," Uffa said.

"Well, get your tickets soon. I hear it's going to sell out. They're going to have a live band. There's going to be an art exhibit, too. Jim Herald is showing fifty years of his bobcat photography."

"Sounds cool," Uffa said.

"Not to be missed, guys. Not to be missed."

"Okay, Walt," they said.

"Take it easy," Walt called, and then he hopped on his bike and rode off into the evening.

CHAPTER 24

SHARKMAN CRIED WHEN HE was honored at the Dance Palace event. He gave a brief speech, in which he thanked all of the elasmobranchologists who came before him and paved the way for his own work. He was wearing a dress shirt and khakis and a pair of polarized sunglasses hung around his neck. Many things in the town were up for debate, but Sharkman's work, it seemed, was universally respected. Everyone from Daryl Shapton to Sharon Lopez to Uffa wanted to shake his hand. There were rumors swirling that he was going to enter the race for District Assemblyman. Uffa believed he would win if he did.

"He appeals to so many different demographics," he explained.

After the award ceremony, there was a raffle. Among the things raffled off were casks of wine from the Shapton Ranch, a three-course meal at Gary's Oysters, and an introductory package at the Korvers' Pilates studio. One of the better prizes was a dory that Alejandro had built. Freddie Moltisanti came away with it.

The money from the raffle would be donated to the Talinas Humane Society and, at the end of the night, Tom Nunes, the organization's director, got up and gave a speech thanking everyone for their contributions. He also let them know about the ongoing animal registration project that the organization was working on.

"We're looking to register animals in the event of a disaster," he said. "We are talking about large animals here, horses or other companion animals. I had a call last week from a woman asking about the tule elk out by Dillon Ranch. This is not for tule elk. We cannot register elk."

During dinner, Walt approached their table and told Uffa and Berg that he could knock down the price of the stadium. As long as they cleaned up everything afterwards, he was willing to rent it to them for a hundred dollars. He felt the town wasn't doing enough to help support its young people, and he wanted to do what he could. After he told them this, he stuck around for a few more minutes to speak to Demeter.

"I've gotta get you and your mom to come do some Pilates with the team," Walt said.

"Oh yeah," Demeter said. "It would be great for their balance."

"I saw that film you acted in with little Petey Johnson," he said. "What a heartrending tale. I felt the emotion, the hurt, the hope to keep the relationship together, despite your character's lack of interest in the Pepper Kings' music. When I saw your mother the other day I told her, I said, 'Demeter's going to be a star.'"

"I don't really want to be a star," Demeter said. "I just want to act and make enough money to survive."

"You're going to be a star," Walt said. "I'm sure of it. Get ready to be a star."

A few days after the Dance Palace event, Berg went out on a Horse Island charter with Garrett and Woody. Woody had picked up most of Berg's shifts by that point. Berg rarely went out on the boat anymore and it was even rarer that he went out with Woody. Berg was still considered a second mate, like Woody, and he was usually paired with someone who was considered a first mate: Simon or Shawnecee, for example. But on occasion they assigned Berg to a charter as a first mate, and that was the case today. He was proud of this, proud of how much he'd learned from Alejandro and Uffa and all of the Fernwood people. He had known nothing when he got there and now he was a first mate.

The client that day was a wealthy man from Denmark named Rasmus. He came with his wife, his thirteen-year-old daughter, and the daughter's best friend. They were on vacation, staying at a bed and breakfast in Five Brooks for the weekend. On the trip over to Horse Island, the two girls posed on the bow, taking selfies and posting them online. Their internet identities and their real lives appeared to have meshed: everything they did was captured for social media and, in many cases, done for the sole purpose of being represented on social media.

"Give me strength," Woody said, shaking his head.

It was around 2:30 p.m. when they left Horse Island and headed back toward Fernwood. The wind was blowing a consistent twenty knots with gusts up to thirty. The tide was ebbing, and the boat bounced across the small, choppy waves. All four passengers were on the foredeck but the girls were no longer taking selfies. In fact, one of them seemed to be feeling sick. She was sitting on the windward side of the boat looking pale and uncomfortable. Then, suddenly, she lurched forward and vomited all over the deck.

"Motherfuck," Garrett said, peering over the dodger with a look of disgust on his face.

This had happened before and Berg knew what to do. He took the fire bucket and dragged it off the stern of the boat, picking up salt water. He would use this water to wash the vomit off the deck and into the bay. But after he'd hauled the bucket up, he turned around to see Woody struggling to furl the jib. The furling line had somehow been released and the jib sheets were whipping around on deck. Garrett was reaching for the sheets, yelling at Woody, and the Danish couple and the two girls were huddled on the foredeck, covering their heads, trying to protect themselves. Berg tied off the fire bucket on a stanchion and rushed over to help Woody with the furling line. As he did so, he jumped up on the cabin top and, moments later, Garrett accidentally jibed.

Berg had not been struck by the boom itself, they all agreed after the fact. If he'd been struck by the boom, he would have been in the water and probably knocked out. And he hadn't been knocked out. He had never lost consciousness. He'd stumbled backward, dazed, and then continued to help Woody furl the jib. Only afterward did he realize how out of it he was. He tried to do some arithmetic in his brain but he felt slow. The water looked strange to him, chaotic in its movements, extra reflective. He must have been struck by the block or the mainsheet, they concluded.

"I'm so sorry," Woody said, once they'd docked and the client had left.

"It's okay, Woody," Berg said.

"Are we going to report this to Mangini?" Garrett said. He was nervous, pacing the galley, clearly afraid that reporting the incident might endanger his job.

"I don't know," Berg said.

"If we're going to report it, we need to report it now."

"I'd say let's report it," Woody said.

"Berg's going to decide," Garrett said. Berg looked at the floor. He felt unable to process what had just happened.

"Let's wait until tomorrow," he said. "I'll see how I feel tomorrow."

CHAPTER 25

IN THE MORNING, WHEN he woke up with blinding headaches, he knew he'd suffered another concussion. It was not as bad as the first one but it was certainly a concussion. Uffa and Demeter drove him to the hospital in Santa Rita, where they took an X-ray of his brain to make sure that he wasn't bleeding internally and then sent him home with a pamphlet about concussions.

Later that afternoon he called Garrett and told him about the concussion. He said he was going to take a week off, that he'd call Mangini to let him know.

"No, no," Garrett said. "Let me talk to Mangini first."

Mangini called Berg fifteen minutes later and told him to take his time recovering. Berg was immediately suspicious: his words sounded inauthentic and forced, as if he were reading them from a teleprompter. Was he just afraid that Berg was going to sue them? He had never trusted Mangini. Nobody trusted Mangini. Berg wondered what Garrett had said to him, why he felt the need to speak to him first.

"The important thing is that we learn from this," Mangini said. "This is a good wake-up call for all of us."

Nell came up to stay with Berg and he spent the next few days in bed, taking ibuprofen and acetaminophen to ward off headaches, with little success. Alejandro and Rebecca let Berg and Nell stay in the guest room in the farmhouse so Berg wouldn't be disturbed by noise from the shop. It was the only spare room in the house and it was simple, unadorned. A small bookshelf and, opposite the bed, a window looking out on the grove of laurels and cedars.

Berg slept and listened to a book on tape about World War II. After three days of rest, he went back to work, for both Alejandro and Mangini. On his first day back, Mangini gave him a weird lecture in which he basically told Berg that the incident was his fault, that he shouldn't have been standing where he was standing, and that he needed to do more sailing training if he wanted to remain at Fernwood.

"We just can't have this happening on charters," Mangini said. "I've been working on the bay for thirty years and this is the most serious accident I've ever been associated with. We've lost trust in you, so you're going to have to earn it back. But I'm glad you're healthy," he added. "You feeling all better?"

"I'm getting some headaches but it's okay."

"Yeah, man, I got smacked in the head all the time when I was younger. You just gotta tough it out. You'll be fine."

It seemed like Mangini had been stewing about the incident for the past three days, demonizing Berg in his absence. Berg was infuriated. The accident had not been his fault. He was not faultless, he shouldn't have been standing there, but there was plenty of blame to go around: Garrett should have never tried to furl the jib in that kind of weather, Woody should have had the line around a cleat, and Garrett shouldn't have accidentally jibed. Still, Berg knew he was lower on the totem pole than Garrett, and he didn't feel like throwing Woody under the bus. He said nothing to Mangini, nodded silently, and then walked down to the docks to prep the boat.

The next two weeks were miserable. The headaches were back and more forceful than ever. They short-circuited his thoughts and they made his whole body feel tense and sensitive, like he'd been drinking a lot of caffeine and not getting any sleep. On occasion, his ears would begin to ring, seemingly at random. He told Alejandro he wasn't doing so well and Alejandro told him he should take more time off.

He did take more time off and felt a little better, but when he went back to work, the headaches returned in full force. He decided he needed to go see another doctor. He had not been inspired to do this earlier, because the specialists he'd seen the first time around had not been helpful. This doctor was no different. He told Berg that there was nothing to do except wait. It was normal to have these kinds of headaches after a concussion, he said, and eventually they would diminish in frequency and intensity.

"Should I be working?" Berg asked.

"It's been what? Over a month?" the doctor said.

"Yeah."

"I don't see why not. You can't make the concussion

symptoms worse at this point," he said. "Just make sure you don't get another one."

So Berg continued to work. But the work he was doing was very poor. They were building out the frames for a skiff for the Moltisanti family, and Berg was helping Alejandro make the auto on the big green bandsaw. Cutting frames was difficult because they had to be cut on a rolling bevel. Berg's job was to push the wood through the saw while Alejandro stood above it, adjusting the bevel as they went. Shortly after they'd started, Berg produced a few unsatisfactory cuts that would have to be fixed with hand tools. He was frustrated because he knew how to do this. It was embarrassing to mess up right in front of Alejandro. Oftentimes, when he made mistakes in the shop, he was allowed to make them in private, and then correct them before he presented the work to Alejandro. But with this work, his teacher was right there, observing.

"It's okay," Alejandro said. "You're not trying to show who you are, you're just trying to make the thing."

Berg nodded. He looked around for Uffa and then remembered that he'd gone over to the farmhouse to begin cooking dinner. Like a college co-op, the family meal was prepared by a different person every night, according to a monthly schedule devised by Rebecca.

"We're just trying to merge with the task at hand," Alejandro said. "That's the best you can do. It's like cooking a meal or walking in a field."

Berg took a deep breath and lifted up the next piece of wood. He'd had a headache all day but it had grown more painful as the day wore on. The more he messed up the cuts, the worse it seemed to get. Right now it was burning white and sharp.

"Are you sure you're okay to do this?" Alejandro asked.

"Yes," he said.

Alejandro watched him for a moment, and then he said, "No." There was a serious look on his face. "No," he said. "C'mon. Here, put this down." He waved at the piece of wood Berg was holding. Berg reared it against the handsaw.

Alejandro led him out of the shop, through the pasture, and into the oak meadow east of the house. They walked for a while until they came to a smooth log. Alejandro sat down on the log and invited Berg to do the same. A soft wind passed through the meadow, carrying with it smells of the distant woods: moist dirt and fir and creek water. Alejandro took a deep breath and then closed his eyes.

"Oh you who are nobly born," he boomed. "Do not forget your true nature."

Berg shifted on the log. He had no idea what Alejandro was up to. He wanted to go home and take six ibuprofen and lie in the cubby. He knew he wouldn't be able to rest well, that the headaches would inevitably disturb him, but it was better than sitting on this log and listening to Alejandro chant sutras, or whatever he was doing.

"That is what the Buddhist texts say," Alejandro continued, more quietly. "Every Buddhist text opens with that address. They seek to remind us of our inherent dignity. Of the wisdom we already possess."

This isn't going to help, Berg thought, but Alejandro's tone was very solemn and he didn't want to be disrespectful, so he sat there, listening.

"Now Berg," he said. "I want you to close your eyes and sit here in a posture that embodies dignity, whatever that means to you."

Berg noticed he had been slouching and sat up straight. He felt more alert after he did this, more engaged.

"And now," Alejandro continued. "I want you to bring your attention to the breath as it moves through the body. Just noticing it. Not trying to alter it, or change anything. Just watching it. And, as the mind creates thoughts, which it inevitably will, just naming them, observing them, and bringing your attention back to the breath."

Berg tried to do this but found it challenging. He couldn't keep his focus on the breath. It was too boring. There was nothing to notice about it. It was like sharpening a chisel, only more difficult and less practical.

"Noticing," Alejandro continued, "if the mind says that it is bored or that it isn't able to do this, and just naming that, and patiently bringing attention back to the breath. What we are trying to do here is cultivate a nonjudgmental awareness. All of our lives we are doing, doing, doing. Constantly judging. And this doing, this judging, it prevents us from seeing what is happening right in front of us."

Berg felt his headache pulsing. That was what was happening right in front of him. He was going to have to tell Alejandro this wasn't working for him, that he needed to go back to the shop. He was strategizing about how he was going to say this, how he was going to tell Alejandro he needed to leave without offending him, when Alejandro spoke again.

"Noticing," he said. "If any pain arises in the body, and just watching that pain, trying to see it for what it is, trying not to push it away. Seeing if, instead of endeavoring to change things, we can just observe what's happening, because it's already here."

After he said this, Alejandro was quiet for several minutes. Berg abandoned his plans of escape and tried, again, to focus on his breathing. He stayed with it for a moment, but then his mind became diverted. It was like a stream rushing down a mountain, forking every time it encountered an obstacle.

Berg was not sure how long they sat in meditation but, after a certain point, he seemed to drop out of clock time. Every so often, Alejandro would provide some kind of instruction.

"Your thoughts and feelings are like weather patterns," he said. "See if you can just watch them pass, not judging them."

When the meditation was over, Berg found that, while his headache hadn't disappeared, it was not as painful as it had been earlier. They walked back to the house and joined the bustle of the kitchen. Marie was baking bread and Uffa was grilling steak. Sandy was in the living room, playing piano and talking to Lizzie at the same time. Rebecca, it seemed, was still out on the farm somewhere. Alejandro poured himself a cup of coffee and a cup of wine. He was the only person Berg had ever met who drank wine and coffee at the same time.

Berg began to clean the table, which was scattered with books and newspaper and glasses of water. Then Tess entered the room. She was wearing overalls, red Converse shoes, and a baseball hat. She had a smudge of dirt under her right eye, a blurry smudge, like a pencil mark that had been rubbed out with a bad eraser. Lately she had been carrying around a small wooden flute and she announced her arrival by wailing on one of its higher notes.

Alejandro put down his drinks, grabbed her, and spun her in the air.

"Pamba," she shrieked. "Stop it!"

Alejandro set her on the ground.

"What did I tell you about inside flute-playing?" he said.

"You didn't say anything about my flute."

"I did."

"This flute?" she said, holding it up.

"That flute."

"This flute?"

Tess brought the instrument very slowly to her mouth as Alejandro stared at her. She blew one sharp note, giggled wildly, and sprinted away.

"Dinner time," Uffa said.

CHAPTER 26

THE DAY OF THE concert, Berg got home late. He'd been out on a sunset charter earlier in the evening with a group of lawyers. He'd had a headache all day and he was feeling irritable, but he really wanted to make it to the show. He'd tried to meditate that week, but he couldn't seem to find the time. Alejandro had mentioned that the meditation would be most useful if he developed a daily practice. But Berg found that it was hard to bring himself to sit. It seemed like there was always something else that took precedence over it.

Woody picked him up after work and the two of them drove over to the stadium. It was just up the road from Albert Worsley's ranch, one of the other properties where Alejandro often milled wood. Worsley, Woody insisted, had also been a part of the drug-rehabilitation cult.

"He was one of the first people I saw when I visited," Woody said. "Greeted me at the entrance with a bunch of other people and had me do the Niebor dance. That was the name of the cult, The Church of Niebor. They made everyone who showed up on their property do the dance right when they got there."

"What was the dance like?"

"You kinda hopped around like a bee. And you made some strange noises. When you finished, they offered you coffee and peanut butter sandwiches. They were always offering you peanut butter sandwiches. They were really into that."

Once inside the stadium, Berg wandered around looking for Nell, who had driven up for the show. The bus was set up near the pitcher's mound and lit with purple and blue light. People crowded around its entrance, drinking beer and smoking cigarettes. Others were sitting in the dugout. Berg recognized very few people. There was a jerry-rigged bar that was decorated with palm fronds and run by a man dressed like a desert nomad. A long piece of elastic blue fabric had been draped from the top of the backstop down to the entrance of the bus, where a young woman with long, bouncy brown hair asked for donations.

"This is a jar of money," she said to no one in particular. "This is a jar of money. Let it be known that this is a jar of money. Do you support vagabond artists? If so, place money in this jar."

Before Berg could find Nell, Uffa called out to the crowd to let them know the show was starting. The side of the bus had been opened like a can, and there was a stage extending out from the opening. Uffa had told Berg that the bus was capable of doing this but he'd never seen it in action.

Everyone gathered in the infield, around the bus. Berg finally located Nell, who was sitting up near the stage, next to two girls with ear gauges and cool haircuts. She waved to Berg and blew him a kiss. She had a green scarf wrapped around her head and she was drinking red wine out of a mason jar.

The first performer hopped up onstage and introduced himself as Maze. He was wearing a denim jacket with a furry collar.

"All right," he said. "Welcome, welcome. Thanks for coming out. It's nice to be out here in the country. Thank you very much to the Oysters for hosting us. We've got Uffa on lights and Chloe on candles. Give them a hand. All right, sorry it's kinda cold out. But this is gonna be some good shit, man. Don't worry. This won't be some shitty concert. This is gonna be some good shit."

Maze sang for about twenty minutes. His songs were about growing up in the Midwest and being a freak and his asshole stepdad who'd fought in Korea. On occasion, he would hum a saxophone solo. At one point he invited Uffa onstage and they sang a song about a boy who looked like a horse. In the middle of the song, Uffa shook his head and neighed like a horse.

After Maze, a red-haired woman came on stage. Her name was Chloe and she sang quiet, brief love songs. Uffa had told Berg about her. She was one of the housemates from the warehouse and Uffa thought he might be in love with her. Berg looked around the audience as Chloe played and noticed that Alejandro and Rebecca were sitting on chairs by second base, holding hands. Rebecca seemed to be enjoying Chloe's music a great deal. Her eyes were closed and there was a gentle smile on her face. More than anyone, though, Walt was loving the show. He was sitting front and center, eyes closed, head bobbing side to side.

When Chloe's set was finished, Uffa announced that there would be a brief intermission and then two closing acts. During the break Berg found himself in line for a drink next to Katherine, of all people.

"Holy shit," he said. "I had no idea you were coming here."

"Yeah!" she said. "I saw that Nell was playing a concert at a minor-league baseball stadium and I thought, How the hell can I miss that? How are you? I hear you're building boats."

"I am," he said. "I live about ten minutes away. With the guy who owns this bus, actually."

They got their drinks and wandered away from the bar. Berg used his beer to swallow a few ibuprofen pills.

"Did you come up alone?" Berg asked.

"Yeah, Eugene had to go to a friend's birthday."

"I miss seeing that guy around."

"He misses you," she said, laughing. "You guys had a sweet friendship."

Berg took another sip of his beer, scanned the surrounding crowd, looking for Nell. The intermission was going to be over soon and he still hadn't had a chance to say hello to her. He wanted to find her before she played. When he looked back at Katherine she had an orange pill bottle out and she was tapping its contents into her hand.

"I have no idea what the fuck I put in here," she said, squinting at the pills in the low light.

By the time the show started up again, Berg was high, soaring high. He'd taken two Perc 30s and an Adderall and he felt euphoric. His headache disappeared and as he watched Nell step up on stage he was filled with a glowing warmth. When she began to play, he found he was finally able to be present, to drop in and really listen. He'd been elsewhere until he took the pills, he realized, skating across the top of every moment, deterred by the pain. Now he was there, absorbed in Nell's performance, and it was extraordinary: keening and poetic and heartful. You could see the audience grow more and more enraptured with each song. She finished her set with the seven-minute ballad about California and her aunt and then the audience roared, stamped their feet. Someone handed Berg a mug of wine. He whistled and cheered, took a gulp of the wine.

When Nell left the stage, Uffa introduced the final act, a guy named Wallace Light. Berg had heard his music before because Uffa played his songs in the shop. He liked what'd he'd heard of the album but Light was even better in person. He played keyboard and guitar and sang out of two different microphones. He looped melodies with a pedal. The energy of the set built and built, and you felt like you were on a plane shrieking down the runway, launching into the air. Most people in the audience seemed to know his music and, during his last song, almost everyone sang along.

"If you chase me I'll run," they sang:

> I'll run into the darkness or the fire
> I won't run forever
> but I'll run a long time
> Force me into a fight
> I'll come at you like the sunlight hits the water
> I won't fight forever
> But I'll fight with my life.

When the show was over, Uffa and Maze began to close up the bus stage. Berg walked over to help them, and right as he got there, Walt appeared.

"I loved it," he told Uffa. "So much light, so much energy. This is the best event this town has seen in a long time. There hasn't been a great show in... I can't remember how long. But we're back. This is so important."

"Thanks, Walt.

"Did you see that news story today about the Canadian government introducing the buffalo back into Banff National Park?"

"No," Uffa said, reaching down to unscrew a leg of the stage.

"Airlifted in these big containers," Walt said. "And the buffalo, sixteen of them, came stampeding back into the park. We wiped out sixty million buffalo but now they're back. That stampede, that was like tonight, man. We're back. What a beautiful show."

When Uffa stood back up, Walt handed him two tickets.

"These are for an Oysters game," he said. "They're on me. Take Ale."

"That's very kind," Uffa said.

Walt gave Uffa a hug and then headed toward the parking lot. Once he was out of sight, Uffa gave Berg both of the tickets.

"I hate baseball," he said.

That night Uffa drove ten people back to the house, mostly friends from the warehouse. Katherine came, too, but she drove over in her own car. They built a fire in front of the bus and then, later, they wandered into the shop. They sat around the workbench, drinking beer and looking up at the boats, their hulls suspended in the air, nodding placidly, like mobiles. Wallace Light was there and Chloe and Demeter. Nell sat on Berg's lap and they all listened to Uffa as he mused, stoned, about his next move. He said he wanted to go to Rome or Bulgaria or maybe Oaxaca. They had connections in Oaxaca. Alejandro had lived in Salina Cruz for a few years while he was studying the Zapotec.

"What do you think about Oaxaca?" he said to Demeter.

"Uffa, I'm going to New York. You know that," she said.

"What do you want with New York?" Uffa said, grinning. "Everyone over there is so uptight. Bunch of worker bees in suits."

"Don't start with me," Demeter said.

Around midnight, they wandered back over to the bus and made popcorn with Uffa's outdoor propane stove. They huddled by the bonfire, drinking wine and eating popcorn and laughing. Eventually, a few people began to leave. Berg saw Katherine say goodbye to Nell and then walk off toward the dark driveway. He hurried after her, his boots squelching in the mud. She was unlocking her station wagon when he caught up to her. They were far away from the party now, and the sound of music and boozy chatter was replaced by the spare sounds of night in Talinas: faint rustlings, hooting owls, silence.

"Hey, it was good to see you," Berg said.

"Oh, you too, Berg," she said, her voice full of warmth and fatigue.

"Just wanted to say bye," he said. "I was also wondering if you could give me Eugene's number? I got a new phone and I lost it."

"Yeah, totally," she said, fishing her phone out of her pocket. "He'd love to hear from you."

CHAPTER 27

IN THE BRIGHT WHITE light of the morning Berg stood beneath the shower, warm water thawing his numb toes. It was summer in Talinas, but there was often fog in summer, a white mist concealing things and then revealing them and then concealing them again, like a man playing peekaboo with a child. When Berg got out of the shower, he checked himself out in the mirror. He looked healthy. Not strung out at all. He'd been using for about three weeks now, but with a couple of exceptions, he was doing a good job holding fast at his maintenance dose. These days that was 200 mg of Tramadol and 10 mg of Adderall. This was similar to the cocktail he'd long taken while working in the city. A pleasurable but highly functional mixture.

He walked back to the cubby and popped the pills. It was going to be a good day. It was Saturday in America and he and Alejandro were heading to the Oysters game. Alejandro was a big Oysters fan, it turned out. When he learned that Berg had been given tickets to a game, he was thrilled.

"Walt gave those to you? Oh, they should be great seats then," he said.

The Oysters, Alejandro explained on the way over, were one of the first teams incorporated into the Far West Division in 1941. Their biggest rivals were, and always had been, the Visalia Rawhide, who, between 1994 and 2009, had been known as the Oaks, but who had recently reverted to their old name after a series of fan surveys and polls. Oysters fans, however, continued to call them the Oaks and Ted Young, owner of Young's Market and arguably the most diehard Oysters fan in Talinas, continued to build a small bonfire of oak branches in front of the stadium before every game versus Visalia, despite repeated requests from the team to cease doing so.

Their seats were on the third-base side and only ten rows away from the field. They found themselves sitting next to Gene Abbott, whom Alejandro introduced to Berg as a mechanic and an "excellent chess player." Gene told Alejandro and Berg that he'd bought the gas station up by the Plains a few months ago.

"I hired Treehouse John to run it," he said.

"I've always liked John," Alejandro said.

"That's the thing. I told him, 'Look John, everyone likes you. Everyone's rooting for you. If you get the drinking under control, I don't see why we can't work together.' And he's doing great. Haven't had any problems. Sometimes his stories get a little tiresome. The other day, for example, he was explaining about why he grew a beard. I said, 'Look John, I don't need to know all the details about your beard.' I mean, it was a long story. Twists and turns and twists and turns." Gene threw his hands in the air. "I just... I mean... who's got the time? It's a man's beard."

The first inning was an unequivocal disaster for the Oysters, who were facing off against Bakersfield that day. Talinas gave up eight runs and had to pull their starting pitcher before he had recorded two outs. Jim Honeywell entered the game as pitcher and forced Bakersfield to ground into a double play to end the inning.

"And with that 6-4-3 double play," the announcer said over the loudspeaker, "the first inning mercifully comes to a close. My gosh. There's just... My gosh. Not a lot to say. Top of the order coming up for the Oysters."

"I like that Honeywell," Gene said to Alejandro. "Good instinct."

The Oysters strung together a few hits in the fourth and Jim Honeywell kept Bakersfield at bay, but by the seventh inning the score was nine to two. People had begun to file out of the stadium. During the seventh-inning stretch, an old man walked onto the field with a cane. He was accompanied by a middle-aged man with a ponytail.

"And now," the announcer said over the loudspeaker. "Please direct your attention toward home plate for another edition of Meet the Candidates, sponsored by Todd's Fish and Tackle. Bring your Oysters ticket into Todd's to receive a discounted copy of Todd's *Advanced Finesse in Fly Fishing* manual. Today, we'd like to welcome Samuel Freisinger, independent candidate for District 4 Assemblyman, and his aide, Rudy Johnson."

Samuel tapped the mic. "Is it on?" he said. "Okay. Here's the thing. Is it on? Okay. Starting over. There's a lot of problems in Talinas. Lots of them. We need a revolution. Declare Talinas a nuclear-free zone. Pardon Edward Snowden. Open relations with Venezuela... What's the... I m missing one..."

"Put Bush on trial," Rudy said.

"That's right," Samuel continued. "Put George W. Bush on trial for war crimes. Free Tibet. Elect the Grateful Dead to the Rock & Roll Hall of Fame, if they have not already been elected by the time I assume office. Encourage vegetarianism. Stop chemtrails. Those are our platforms. We want you to turn out this November. We need your vote. My name is Samuel Freisinger. Please visit my website at SamuelFresinger.blogspot.com, where I elaborate on my positions. We cannot wait any longer. Our time is now. Thank you."

There was a light smattering of applause throughout the stadium. Samuel walked over to the dugout, where he donned an Oysters hat and waved to the crowd.

The Oysters gave up two more runs and did not score any themselves. By the eighth inning, the announcer could barely conceal his disappointment.

"A swing and a miss from Ricky Rogers," he said. "And the strikeouts for the Oysters continue to mount. Fourteen strikeouts on the day. And you just have to wonder what... oh whatever, here's Davey Knittles to the plate with two down and no one on."

It was around 3 p.m. when they left. The sun was high in the sky and the air smelled like caramel corn and hot dogs. As Berg and Alejandro walked through the parking lot, they discussed their plans for the rest of the day. Maybe they would go swimming at Jensen Beach or take out the *Contos*. And then they saw

Lammy approaching them. She was wearing a shawl and large, circular earrings that looked like dream catchers.

"Lammy," Alejandro said. "Good to see you."

"I've got bad news," she said.

"Oh no."

"Pat's been arrested," she said.

"Oh no."

"In San Diego. All three of them were apprehended."

"What about JC?"

"He's gone. He left for Mexico last night. I don't know where exactly. He didn't want me to know."

She seemed like she might cry.

"Are you safe?" Alejandro asked.

"I'm going to my mother's in Sacramento. I'll be fine there."

"Do we need to go somewhere?"

"No, you should be okay," she said. "You know what to say if anyone asks about the boats."

"I can't believe this is happening."

"I've got to go, Ale."

"Okay, take care, Lammy," he said.

On the ride home Alejandro ranted about JC. He'd been cutting corners for years now, he said, trying to expand too quickly. All the success had gone to his head and he thought he was invincible and now he'd endangered all of them. His kids, Lammy, Pat and his crew, not to mention Alejandro's own shop and family.

"Can you get by without his commissions?" Berg asked.

"It's possible," he said. "We have before. It's a lot more difficult. But frankly that's the last of my worries right now. I just hope I don't end up on trial."

CHAPTER 28

AS LAMMY PREDICTED, THE police did not come for Alejandro. Still, most days, he refused to leave the farm. He didn't want to run into anyone in town and be forced to answer questions about JC and Pat. Uffa thought he was being paranoid but Berg didn't find it unreasonable. Rumor of Pat's apprehension had spread throughout the town and everyone was talking about it.

Holed up on the farm, Alejandro spent most days putzing around, helping Rebecca in the fields and baking bread with Marie. All work on JC's sloop came to a halt and, as a result, Uffa decided to take a trip in the bus with Demeter. They wanted to go visit the warehouse in Oakland and then head through the Southwest.

"I've got some survival tickets stored up," he said. "Time to hit the road."

Berg, for his part, began picking up more shifts at Fernwood. There were a lot of charters happening and Garrett was eager to have him back. Unsurprisingly, Garrett and Simon were obsessed with the details of Pat's arrest. Both of them seemed to think Berg knew more than he was letting on, and they pressed him for information.

"I heard JC's heading down there to spring them," Simon said.

"Who told you that?" Berg said.

"That new girl at the bakery."

"Simon, stop it with your conspiracies," Garrett said. "Berg would tell us if that was the case. Wouldn't you, Berg?"

"I guess," Berg said.

"Why would JC risk his neck to go spring those guys, Simon?" Garrett said.

"So they don't rat on him," Simon said.

"Pat won't rat, Simon. He won't. I know that dude. He's a tough Texas hombre."

"All I know is it took Deputy White two minutes to get Cal to rat on Lee Kearns last year."

"For the thing with the tractor?"

"That's right," Simon said. "The police have sophisticated techniques. That's all I'm saying."

"Simon, what I'm saying is you have no idea what you're talking about."

Berg didn't tell Garrett and Simon anything, but he did know some things. He knew Pat had been caught while stopping to reprovision the ship in San Diego. He knew that the police had confiscated nearly eleven thousand pounds of pot and that Pat and his crew were facing ten-year sentences. He knew that Lammy had been interrogated in Sacramento and he knew that JC had made it down to Mexico without incident. According to Lammy, he was hiding out in Michoacán somewhere. It was not clear if and when he would be able to return.

Those few weeks after the arrest were dark ones, but they also seemed to bring everyone closer. Berg helped out with the farm and he got to know Rebecca better. He also became closer with Alejandro's son, Sandy, who took Berg fishing in his little dory. He was fifteen years old, a strange young man who read ancient Eastern epics and tried, unsuccessfully, to hunt with a bow and arrow that he'd built himself. Berg liked him: he was open-minded and smart and unpredictable. Once, while they were out on the water, he told Berg that he considered him a member of the family. Berg was surprised by how good it made him feel.

By the end of the month, Alejandro seemed to be in a better mood. He started making trips to town again and seemed less fearful of interacting with people. He and Berg started construction on a wine cellar near Lizzie and Jens's cabin, and as they worked, Alejandro began to explain his plans for the future of the shop, which clearly he'd been ruminating on for the last month. Without the revenue from JC, they'd need to make a pivot, he said, but there were lots of opportunities for them. His favorite idea had to do with the production of canoes. Years ago, he had designed an affordable two-plank canoe. It was a simple design and he planned to construct it entirely out of coastal fir, which grew in abundance around the farm.

"We could use a spongier wood for the spline," he said.

"Maybe we use cedar or something to prevent the spline from breaking, but other than that it's just fir."

Alejandro called it the twenty-four-hour canoe because he could build one, alone, in twenty-four hours. Apparently he had timed himself doing this several years ago. He insisted that Berg and Uffa could also produce one of these boats in twenty-four hours, though Berg doubted this. The main idea was to build out these canoes and rent them to tourists on the bay. There were a few kayak and canoe rental places operating, but none of them used wooden boats. Alejandro thought people would see these boats on the water and prefer them. Over time, they'd build up a small fleet of rental canoes, which would provide a steady base-level income for the shop, and then, on occasion, they could sell them off for a thousand dollars if anyone inquired about purchasing one.

"We'll mill the fir ourselves," he said. "We'll build one boat per day. We can even build them out on the beach, right behind the house, so people going by on the ferry will see them. It will be free advertising."

Another part of his plan was the construction of a 3-D ocean-farming system, which he had read about online. The goal, he explained, was to produce a vertical sea garden, anchored by oyster traps. The ropes of the traps would grow seaweed and mussels and there would be clams beneath the oyster traps. It was very environmentally sustainable, he explained, because it required no feed, no water, and no fertilizer. They could harvest sea salt, too, and dry it in the greenhouse. Berg asked Alejandro where he'd read about all of this.

"Forums," he said, without elaborating.

The third prong of Alejandro's scheme was a weekend boat-building class. The class would consist of about nine students, and they would meet on Saturday, all day, and learn the basics of wooden boat construction. Most of them would never learn anything more complex than mortise and tenon but that was okay. Apparently, Alejandro had taught a class like this back in the '80s and it had been popular. Morty Weisenstein, the local DJ, had been his first student. This was back when the Morrises had convinced Morty that he was a Venutian.

"That was a strange time for him, spiritually speaking," Alejandro said. "He did great in the class, though. Made a nice hollowing plane."

Before any of these operations got underway, however, they were distracted by different projects. The first one came in the form of John Coleman, knocking at the door of the farmhouse during dinner, begging for help. Coleman said his boat had begun to take on water and he didn't know why. He was worried. He needed someone to fix it but he had no money.

"And why would I help you?" Alejandro asked.

"Well, I've asked all the other boatbuilders and you're the only one left."

"How would you eventually be able to pay me?"

"I'd be able to pay you because I'd be able to fish again."

Berg didn't know Coleman, but he knew the stories about him. Back when Berg was a nightly drinker at the Tavern, he'd listened to more than one man complain about the debt John Coleman owed him. But Alejandro decided to give Coleman the benefit of the doubt and, the following morning, he asked Berg to come with him to Vlasic's Boat Works.

"What are we doing?"

"We're fixing John Coleman's boat," Alejandro said.

Vlasic was not around that morning when they arrived. Technically they should have waited for him to return before hauling out, but Alejandro was impatient and did it anyway. After briefly inspecting the boat, he noticed that the garboard plank seemed poorly fastened. He took it with one hand and ripped the whole thing off.

"There's the problem," he said.

The two of them worked throughout the morning but there was still no sign of Vlasic. During lunch, Coleman invited Berg into the galley of his boat to eat. Alejandro had driven home to eat lunch with Rebecca and to check on one of the cows, who he said had something funny going on with her knee. In the galley, Coleman opened his refrigerator and asked Berg if he wanted a hamburger. Berg could tell by the smell emanating from the refrigerator that Coleman's hamburger meat was rancid, and he told him so.

"This meat?" Coleman said, taking a handful of the raw chuck in his hand and holding it up for Berg to inspect.

"Yes."

Coleman shrugged and put the raw meat in his mouth, chewed, and swallowed. "No, it's fine," he said.

"I think I'm going to go get a sandwich from Gary's next door."

"Suit yourself."

When Berg returned from Gary's Oysters, he found Vlasic screaming at Coleman. Daryl Shapton and Jim Moltisanti were standing by, having recently hauled out the catboat they co-owned.

"What are you doing, Coleman?" Vlasic yelled. "The boat has to go back in the water. It's blocking one of my main railways!"

"The plank was ripped off," Coleman said. "It will sink."

Alejandro had just pulled up in his truck and was headed toward the railway.

"Who ripped off the plank?" Vlasic said. He looked around and saw Alejandro approaching. "Did you do this?" he said.

"Mr. Vlasic," Alejandro said. "We'll have this finished in four days."

"Not a chance."

"We will."

"You're out of your mind. You think you can just bring my whole business to a stop?"

"I promise you," Alejandro said.

"This what you do now?" Vlasic sneered. "Now that your whole criminal operation got shut down? You come over here and gum up my railways? I'm calling the Coast Guard to get this thing out of here."

"It would be illegal to launch it now," Alejandro said. "The boat would sink."

"I'm calling the Coast Guard," he repeated.

"Call them," Alejandro said. "They won't launch the boat. It would be illegal."

Vlasic scowled. He knew he had no other options.

"Four days, Vega," he said. "And your haul-out rate is doubled."

"You can't just double the price," Alejandro said.

"Watch me!" Vlasic roared. Then he turned and disappeared into the shop's office.

For the next few days they worked eighteen-hour days fixing Coleman's boat. Coleman helped, running to the hardware store to pick up things they needed. The whole time they worked, Alejandro grumbled about Vlasic and his family.

"They are so small-minded," he said to Berg. "Very parochial."

Berg liked the pace of the labor, liked having boat work to

do again. He upped his dose of Adderall and switched over to Oxys, which always gave him more energy. He made sure to keep his dose consistent and mild during the week. He didn't want to get too high and chop his finger off with a circular saw. The only problem was the constipation: his stomach often felt bloated and his bowel movements were, once again, irregular and uncomfortable. He tried to make a note to drink extra water and eat fibrous things, but the problem persisted. He was going to quit soon anyway, he reasoned. Once this stash he'd bought from Eugene ran out, he wouldn't re-up. Then it would just be a matter of dealing with the withdrawal, like last time.

After four days of work, they had replaced a long section of the keel and put on new garboard planks. When they relaunched the boat, Vlasic was in town picking up lunch. Berg had been waiting for the moment when Alejandro would say goodbye to Vlasic, when he'd point out that he'd been able to complete the work in four days. But Alejandro seemed uninterested in sticking around for this moment of righteous vindication. They packed up their stuff and headed toward the road. On their way out they bumped into Terry Strauss. He ran a construction company in town. Berg knew who he was because he worked with Dennis Lapley, the addict Berg used to hang out with at the Tavern.

"You guys did it," Terry said. "Damn."

"Yep, she's back out there," Alejandro said.

"And you did that for Coleman?" he said, laughing. "Good luck getting paid for that."

CHAPTER 29

BUT COLEMAN DID BEGIN to pay Alejandro back. That fall he brought weekly installments over to the house, along with a few fish from the day's haul. Based on the wide variety of fish Coleman brought over, Alejandro assumed that the fish were being caught in a questionable manner. He suspected that Coleman was using a beach seine, a fishing method that Alejandro had practiced himself, back in the day, before it was deemed illegal. He asked Coleman if he was doing this, and Coleman denied it. In the end, Alejandro decided not to press the issue.

Shortly thereafter, Alejandro received a call from Celia, an old friend in Pine Gulch. She wanted to commission him to build a sloop. Alejandro considered turning down the job. He wanted to get started on the sea-farming project, but Celia was offering a lot of money, and she was a friend, so he decided to go ahead with it.

Celia wanted the boat to be capable of cruising but she also wanted to be able to put it on a trailer. Alejandro designed a twenty-eight-foot lapstrake, a double-ender, with a nine-and-a-half-foot beam and a six-foot draft. It would be a swift boat, Scandinavian in style and reminiscent of a Spidsgatter. He planned to use the leftover pepperwood from JC's sloop for the planking and oak for the sawn frames.

When he was done with the design, Alejandro let Berg help him with the lofting.

"Most people hate lofting," he told Berg. "But I've always loved it."

Alejandro did all of his designing and lofting by hand, using long wooden battens to draw fair lines. It required a meticulous focus, but it rewarded you for that focus. There was nothing more satisfying than making a slight alteration and watching that alteration ripple through the rest of the design, relieving it of its imperfections.

When the lofting was finished, Alejandro called Uffa and asked him if he could move back to help them with the boat. He came clattering into Alejandro's backyard the next day at 11 p.m.

"I drank three 5-hour Energy drinks to get here," he said. "I was down in Joshua Tree." Berg and Alejandro were in the living room, reading. Rebecca and the others had gone to bed a couple of hours ago.

"Why do you drink those?" Alejandro asked, standing up to hug him.

"It's like Adderall," he said, embracing Alejandro. "Makes everything easier. It's basically just Adderall you can buy in a store."

"I've never tried an Adderall," Alejandro said.

"Don't," Uffa said. "You're like eighty years old. You'd probably have a heart attack."

Uffa walked into the kitchen and began rifling through the pantry. "You have any cereal? Or like a bagel or something?" he asked.

"There's some leftover cheese and bread," Alejandro said.

"Excellent."

Uffa took a hunk of bread and cheese and came back into the living room.

"Where's Demeter?" Berg asked.

"Dropped her at her mom's before I came here," he said. "You guys hear anything about Pat and JC?"

"The trial is dragging on," Alejandro said. "But they're looking at ten years."

"Fuck. For real?" Uffa said. "That's messed up."

"It's terrible. But they haven't been convicted yet. I'm hoping they've got good lawyers."

"What about Lammy?"

"She seems to be okay. And we haven't heard anything from JC. He's still in Mexico."

"Damn, man. That drug is going to be legal in like two years, too."

"But it's not legal yet," Alejandro said.

When Uffa finished his snack, Alejandro took out the sketch of the new boat. He talked about the kinds of wood he wanted to use and the amount of time he thought the project would take. Uffa examined the lines.

"So the cylinder's tilted this way?" he asked.

"No, it's tilted this way," Alejandro said. "You're looking straight down."

"And this is the radius? Where does it cross the buttock lines? Ah, right here, I see."

When they were done looking at the lines, Berg helped Uffa move the bus behind the shop. There was a slight incline and it was a delicate process, especially at night. As Uffa backed in, Berg held his cell phone light in the air, directing him like an air traffic controller. Once they were done, Uffa said he needed to go to sleep. Berg hugged him and said goodnight, but before he turned to leave, Uffa stopped him.

"You doing all right?" he said.

"You mean because of all the JC stuff?" Berg said. "Naw, I'm not worried about that."

"No, I mean, how are you doing? You look a little… I don't know, you look different."

"I'm just tired," Berg said.

"Just tired," Uffa nodded.

"Yeah, we were working on Coleman's boat for such long hours and I feel like I still haven't caught up on sleep."

"Oh, okay. Well go get some rest then."

"I will."

"It's good to see you, Berg."

Before going up into the cubby he stopped in the shop bathroom. He turned on the light and examined himself in the mirror, something he hadn't done since the day of the Oysters game. The eggplant-colored depressions under his eyes had returned and he had lost weight. This part was strange, because it seemed like he was eating three square meals a day with the family. He had no explanation for it. Maybe he had a tapeworm, or maybe he wasn't eating as much as he thought he was.

When Berg got to the cubby he lifted up his mattress and examined his dwindling stash. Maybe fifteen Oxys and twenty Perc 30s. Lots of Adderall. When the opioids ran out it was over, he told himself. This time it was finally over. He could deal with the headaches. They probably wouldn't even be that bad anymore. It had been months since the second concussion.

CHAPTER 30

BERG'S FAVORITE TIME TO be in the shop was mid-afternoon, a couple of hours after they took their lunch. Around that time Alejandro would disappear and return with espressos for Uffa, Berg, and himself. The three of them would sit around the work-table and drink the espressos and talk and the air would smell like cedar or pepperwood or whatever they'd been cutting.

By the time they returned to work, Berg felt light, energetic. He always did his best work during these hours. He would be at the bench, working the wood, teasing it into the shape he needed, and maybe Uffa would be cutting a joint for the cabin top or riveting a plank, and Alejandro would be up on the loft floor, corroborating the arc of a new diagonal, humming some Mexican folk song. On occasion you would hear the roar of a sports car speeding down the 1 or the shouts of the oystermen out on the bay. Perhaps Swallow would wander into the shop for a drink of water, before resuming her harassment of the local squirrel population. If she did, they rarely noticed her. It was mid-afternoon, and they were absorbed in their work.

One of these afternoons found them resawing pepperwood for the planking of Celia's boat. The stem for the boat had been cut, along with the grown knees. Alejandro had finished the transom and attached it to the sternpost. It stuck up in the air in the center of the shop like the fluke of a whale.

The tree they'd found that day on Al Garther's property was very large and would provide them with more than enough wood for Celia's boat. It had a beautiful marbled quality, and resawing it felt like cutting into a fresh side of beef. When they were almost done with the work, Alejandro asked Berg to go into town to pick up some plywood. They'd need it for tomorrow, when they would begin spiling the first planks.

Birds called from all sides as he walked to the truck, bright sky, bright sun, a fine warm day. The road to town was the same as it ever was: winding, mostly empty, the bay on his left, the green hills on his right, smooth and rolling, punctuated on occasion by an oak tree or a ragged cypress. And below it all, he thought, the trap door of geologic plates, likely to slip at some point, but for now holding their own.

Before picking up the plywood, Berg decided he would stop in at the bakery for a cookie. The bakery was run by Leonora Spinetta, an older woman who lived near Bear's Landing. She was generally a nice person but she had a temper. Berg had seen her brandish a bread knife at three boys who had allegedly kicked their soccer ball into the bakery's screen door. Some people said she was descended from the Lanza crime family in the city, but Berg had no idea if this was true.

At the bakery, Berg found himself in line with Freddie Moltisanti. He recognized Berg and said hello.

"You're the new guy at Vega's place, right?"

"Yeah, Freddie, right?"

"That's right. Hey, he still making those soaps?"

"Soaps?"

"Yeah, the shampoos and stuff. Him and his boys used to sell them in town."

"Oh, no... not anymore," Berg said.

"Damn," Freddie said. "Those were good soaps, man. I liked those soaps."

Berg thought about Alejandro's new schemes. He wondered if they were in any way viable, or if they'd die off like his cosmetics enterprise. It was hard to say, but in the end, he trusted Alejandro. His mind seemed to be always on the border of madness, but it never fully went over the edge. Or maybe it did. Maybe it could. Berg didn't really know.

As Berg left the coffee shop, he heard someone calling his name. He assumed it was Freddie, but when he looked to his right, he was surprised to see Dennis Lapley, the addict he used to sit next to at the Tavern.

"Berg, hey, Berg."

He was sitting at a picnic table, drinking a beer.

"Come over here, man," Lapley said. "I haven't seen you in forever."

Berg walked over to him and Lapley extended his hand.

"Berg, my buddy. Take a seat, man. Take a seat."

"I'm good," Berg said. "Need to stop in the hardware store."

"C'mon man, take a seat. What's the rush? Haven't seen you in forever."

Berg obliged him. Lapley sniffed, began talking about how he ran into Billy White the other day. Lapley said White had bitched for hours about Garrett and Fernwood, how they had narced on him and wrecked his charter business.

"I thought of you," Lapley said. "You still work at Fernwood, right?"

"Sometimes," Berg said.

"Man, well don't tell Billy that. Dude is pissed."

"Don't know why I would," Berg said. "Never see him."

There was a pause, then Lapley said,

"Hey, I've been meaning to run into you. I got a bunch of this new stuff that I'm trying to deal off."

He took a big pill bottle out of his backpack and poured a few of the pills into his hand. They were round and dark blue, bruise-colored.

"Now, you know me," he said. "I don't usually take pills. But this shit is good, man. I love this shit."

"It's fentanyl," Berg said.

"Oh, you know it? Yeah, I forgot the name, but yeah, that's what the dude said…"

Berg stared at the pills, felt the dragon breathing inside him.

"I'll take the whole thing," Berg said.

"What? The whole thing? I don't even know if I want to sell all of this off…"

"Well, I'll take however much you want to sell off."

"Okay, for sure," Lapley said. "You're gonna dig this shit."

"Let me go to the ATM," Berg said. "I'll be back in a second."

On the drive home, he thought about throwing the pills out

the window, but he could not bring himself to do it. It was a vague thought, uncentered, and rooted in nothing. He felt totally disconnected from his emotions, from any sense of responsibility to himself or to others. All he wanted to do was take the pills. And that was what he was going to do.

Later that evening, alone in the cubby, he poured out several of the pills on his bedside table. As he leaned back, waiting for the rush to hit him, he thought about how he had broken into Alejandro's house when he first moved to Talinas. He had tried to forget this fact, but it had not disappeared. It had moved from his mind to his body, where it remained, tightly coiled, one of those trapped thoughts that expressed itself only on rare occasions in the form of an eye twitch or a watery stomachache.

He thought about what would happen if Alejandro learned the truth. As he imagined this, something released in him, and the extent of his duplicity became clear. It was everywhere, impossible to separate, like flour mixed with salt. A deep, black panic welled in his chest. He wanted the fentanyl to kick in but it wasn't hitting him. Maybe it was extended-release, he thought.

He ground up a few more pills to remove the extended-release coating, arranged them in neat lines on his bedside table. Wait a second, he thought. Give it one more second. Don't be an idiot. He looked out the small square window at the bay. The water was green like an apple, lit with rich evening light. But the panic in his chest wouldn't leave. He couldn't take it. He turned and snorted each line. This was going to take him way deep, he knew, but that was what he needed. He wanted to go all the way to the bottom, to scoop up its brown muck and hold it in his hands. At least then he would know where he was.

CHAPTER 31

WHEN HE WOKE UP, his body was lit with pain. A pulsing, seething, freezing, ungodly pain. He had no idea where he was. He was on his back but where was he?

"I don't know why you fools snort this shit," someone said.

He writhed on the hospital bed, squeezing his eyes open and shut, clenching his teeth. He saw Uffa in the corner of the room. He was looking on in horror, face wet with tears, his purple bandanna sagging around his neck. Berg began to sneeze and, after one of these sneezes, he told them he was freezing cold. Uffa asked the nurse to bring him another blanket. The nurse draped the blanket over Berg and then Berg began to cry, to wail.

"The naloxone triggers immediate withdrawal," the doctor explained.

"It's so bad," Berg cried. "It's so bad."

Alejandro was there, too.

"You'll be all right," he kept saying. "You'll be all right."

Berg gasped for air. He tried to sit up but couldn't. His center of gravity was off. His vision was blurry. There was a faint taste of blood in his mouth, a metallic taste, like he'd been sucking on a penny. The pain was so bad he wanted to smash his head on a rock.

"Remember this," the doctor said. "Remember this feeling the next time you reach for that garbage."

"You assholes gave it to me," Berg growled.

"I didn't give you anything," the doctor said. "And I sure as hell didn't make you snort it."

"Fuck you," Berg said.

"Give him more lorazepam," the doctor said.

The nurse came over and did something to his IV.

"I know this is painful," she said. "You're experiencing full withdrawal right now."

"I'm going to vomit," Berg said.

She handed him a plastic basin. He heaved into it and then passed it back to her. He was sweating now, but he was also shivering. It made no sense. Alejandro walked over and put his hand on his shoulder.

"Don't touch me," Berg said. "What did you do to me?"

"You did this," the doctor said. "No one did this to you."

"Is this normal?" Alejandro asked the doctor.

"Patients are always combative after the naloxone," the nurse said.

"I think I'm dying," Berg said. "I'm dying."

"You're not dying," the doctor said. "We just saved your life."

"Fuck you," Berg said. "Fuck this guy."

The pain was an ascending arpeggio, a madness. Berg had broken many bones in his life, had snapped his tibia all the way through, and nothing compared to this. As the pain reached its most unbearable peak, he felt himself going into shock. The agony ceased. The pain was still there, but it was as if his body would not allow him to feel it. He stared wide-eyed at Alejandro and in a calm, collected voice, he asked,

"Is this real?"

Then he passed out.

CHAPTER 32

HE DID NOT KNOW how long he slept, but when he woke, the acute pain had subsided. He turned to his right and saw Alejandro. He was sitting in a plastic chair, drinking coffee from a Styrofoam cup and watching TV. It was local news. Channel four.

"Good morning," he said, turning to Berg.

"Morning," Berg said. He looked at Alejandro for a moment, and then trained his gaze on the television. He stared, blinking, as the news anchor ran through the day's headlines. Someone had won millions of dollars in the mega-jackpot lottery. A thawed reindeer carcass was being blamed for an anthrax outbreak. Stock prices had risen and fallen and then risen again.

"Would you like a coffee?" Alejandro asked, watching him. Berg shook his head.

"Some food?"

"No."

There was a whirring noise coming from some unidentifiable location. Outside he could hear the hiss and squirt of a sprinkler. Berg felt sore and weak and the more conscious he became, the more ashamed he felt. Fragments of memory returned to him, the foul things he'd said. He needed to apologize to the nurse and the doctor. He needed to apologize and then flee this place. He never wanted any of these people to see his face again.

"You're going to be okay," Alejandro said.

"I don't know," Berg said.

"Just deal with today," Alejandro said. "All you can do is deal with today."

"Why are you here?" Berg asked.

Alejandro took a sip of his coffee.

"I'm here because I care about you," he said.

"I'm an asshole. I'm a fucking drug addict asshole who screams at doctors."

"That was the naloxone. That wasn't you."

"You don't even know me," Berg said. "You don't. I'm not who you think I am."

"Well tell me who you are then."

Berg said nothing.

"Berg, you are very lucky," Alejandro continued. "That's what I'm thinking right—"

"I stole things," Berg said, interrupting him. "I stole things from people's homes. From your home. I lied to you, I lied to Nell."

"Okay."

"So now you know."

"Now I know," Alejandro said.

"Do you know what I stole?"

"I could make an educated guess."

Berg stared at him.

"Oh stop," Alejandro said. "You think your pain makes you so special and complicated? That there's something so crazy about you? There isn't."

"I lied…"

"And?"

Berg said nothing.

"You just need to come back to this world, to the truth of things," Alejandro said. His voice was fierce. "Right now. Do it now."

Berg looked out the window at a brown rooftop. They were on the second floor. Next door he could hear the nurses helping treat a new patient. She'd sprained her ankle while hiking that morning, it seemed. The smell of hospital was everywhere: plastic and disinfectant and urine. He wanted to go home.

"I'm sorry," he said, looking back toward Alejandro. "I'm sorry." He was crying, shaking slightly. Alejandro walked over to him and put his hand on his shoulder. Berg could feel a growing tightness in his forehead and his jaw. A headache was brewing, gathering force by the moment, its clouds condensing. It would be upon him in no time.

CHAPTER 33

HE DIDN'T WANT TO go to an inpatient rehab center. And he didn't want to mess with Suboxone or carpet-bomb his brain with antidepressants. He would go to the meetings in Pine Gulch and work with Alejandro. He'd delete Eugene's number from his phone again, and he'd stay away from Dennis Lapley.

"Pine Gulch is a forty-five-minute drive from here," Nell said. They were sitting in the bakery in town.

"I know, but I'll make it work," Berg said.

"Don't you think it might make sense to live somewhere closer to treatment centers?" she asked. "Somewhere closer to a hospital?"

"I want to keep working with Alejandro," Berg said.

"What does he think about that?"

"He's okay with it."

"I don't know," Nell said, unconvinced.

"I have the Narcan spray now. So does Alejandro. And I'm not going to relapse, anyway," he said.

"I can't believe we're still dealing with this."

"I understand that you're mad at me," he said. "You have every right."

"I'm just really sad, Berg," she said. "It's just… it's sad. And it's scary. I'm scared for you."

The first day back in the shop he could barely look at Alejandro and Uffa. He kept his head down, cut blocks for the rigging and then soaked them in warm linseed oil in Alejandro's old white Crock-Pot. Uffa asked him if he wanted to go out on the *Contos* after work but he said no. He went straight to his bed in the cubby and read a novel.

The following day he did the same thing: cut blocks and soaked them in linseed oil. He ate lunch alone, down by the water, and thought about the hospital, about the way he had screamed at the doctor. He had no appetite but he forced himself to finish his lunch. Leftover chicken from last night's dinner and a small salad. It tasted like nothing.

When the day was over, Alejandro told Berg to follow him outside.

"Come on," he said. "We're going for a walk."

"I don't want to meditate," Berg said.

"We're not going to meditate. We're just going for a walk."

Berg set down his chisel and followed him out of the shop. They walked along the path, down toward Mimi's. Miner's lettuce along the trail and wrens in the branches. Alejandro turned right and headed into the forest. The sun was setting, the cool evening coming, with its mosquitoes and hysterical coyotes. They walked in silence, rustling through the forest. At one point Berg almost stepped on a banana slug. It was the size of a highlighter, oozing with yellow-green slug slime. Then Alejandro spoke.

"When Szerbiak died it devastated me," he said. "He was my brother. I hated him for dying. I hated him. For a long time I couldn't look at his death at all. I threw myself into my work, you see? The farm, the boats." He sighed. "I looked away. But I know I need to sit with it. Just like I've had to sit with all the hardest things in my life. You see, no one taught me about that. No one taught me to look at the darkness, to sit with it. But you've got to go into it. If there's one thing I've learned, it's that you've got to go into it. That doesn't mean you sanction it. That doesn't mean you say you like it. It just means that you look at it, that you acknowledge that it's there—because it already is."

He stopped walking and turned around to face Berg.

"Soon you're going to be old like me—"

"Ale…"

"No, no, let me wax poetical for a second. Have I ever waxed poetical at you?"

"Yes."

"Okay, well let me do it again. Soon you're going to be old like me and I guarantee you, the one thing I don't ever wish is that I'd worried more. Not one day do I wake up and say, 'Gee, I wish I'd spent more time being afraid.' No, I just wish I'd looked at things head-on. Because anxiety needs the future. If you're looking at the thing itself it's very unlikely you'll be anxious."

"But what if the thing itself is ugly?"

"Well, then it's ugly. But the suffering happens when you try to make it not ugly when it's ugly. I'm not saying it's easy. I fail at it all the time. But it's the only way."

They walked past several tan oaks and pepperwoods, into the shade of a few Douglas firs. The fir needles were soft under their feet, the light fading now.

"Should we turn around?" Berg asked.

"Sure, let's turn around."

They said nothing on the walk home, just watched the forest, listened to its evening murmurings. When they got back to the house Alejandro embraced Berg in front of the shop.

"There's more right with you than wrong with you," he said. "Remember that." And then he turned and hobbled off toward his house.

Berg climbed the ladder to the lofting floor and crawled into the cubby. Through the small square window he watched the stars come out over the bay. He leaned back in his bed. He hadn't eaten dinner, he realized. It didn't matter. He wasn't hungry.

CHAPTER 34

PAT WAS CONVICTED THAT winter. Eighty-two months in custody for smuggling eleven thousand pounds of pot into California. "We aren't going to let our oceans become a freeway for drug traffickers," the prosecuting attorney said in the news. "Smugglers might think the vast Pacific is a good place to be invisible, but these defendants know otherwise."

"It's an outrage," Alejandro said to Berg, after reading the article. "You've got corporations polluting our rivers and mountains and air with impunity. You've got hedge fund managers manipulating the global economy. The stock market is just pure thought—you know that, right? When we run out of thoughts it will cease to exist. Those guys are scamming everyone and Pat, who's doing something that harms no one, who's delivering medicine—and delivering it without using any fossil fuels, I might add—he's the guy who goes to prison."

That same winter, Nell went on tour with Carlos Carlos de Carlos again. Berg wrote her letters almost every week, simple notes about his day-to-day, about life in the shop. He'd aim the letter toward whatever city they were visiting next, but he was never sure if they'd make it.

Sometimes, the shame of his lies, of his exposure, of his OD, would be so strong that his chest would hurt. He'd write Nell a long letter about how worthless he was and how much he'd fucked up, and then he'd crumple that letter up and throw it out. She didn't need his self-pity. She needed him to show up, to maintain some kind of consistent, base-level integrity.

The headaches were still there. He knew they would be. They came on an almost daily basis, and when they did, if he could summon the courage to do so, he welcomed them. He tried to watch them, moment by moment, to observe their texture and sensation, to avoid pushing them away.

Berg was not the only one having a difficult time that winter. Uffa was experiencing his own tailspin. Demeter had purchased a ticket to New York and, in less than a month, she would be moving across the country. When Uffa first heard the news, he spent a week alone in his room, recording an elegiac freestyle rap album. Later, he adopted a gray stray cat and named him Grayman.

"I think he dips his giant mouth scoop into multiple food bowls around town," Uffa said. "But he likes to sleep on the bus now."

With Celia's boat almost finished, Alejandro had turned once again to his three-pronged plan to generate extra revenue. He spent all day at the docks, puttering around and experimenting with his first 3-D ocean-farming structures. He had built several different kinds and he wanted to test their efficacy over time.

Meanwhile, in the shop, Berg was attempting to build his first twenty-four-hour canoe. It was taking him a lot longer than twenty-four hours, but this morning, after a week of work, he was finally ready to fasten the first plank. He looked around the shop for the specialized jig Alejandro had made to rivet the canoes, but he couldn't find it.

As he walked down to the docks he could hear the creaking of pilings, the jabber of gulls. When he got to the water, he found Alejandro on the ground, examining kelp.

"It probably makes most sense to dry out this kelp," Alejandro said, looking up at Berg. "That way we can sprinkle it over our crops as a fertilizer. It would close the nitrogen loop, you know? The kelp would sop up the nitrogen and then we'd use it to grow our vegetables and then it would make its way back into the bay. The issue is the smell. It has an unfortunate odor. Rebecca hates it. Maybe I could mix it in a solution with something else to minimize the odor? Or maybe I should just scrap the whole fertilizer idea and sell the seaweed to high-end restaurants? That would probably make us the most money anyway."

Alejandro went on in this manner, discussing the different contingencies of his kelp situation. His mind seemed scattered, burnt out, overheated like a computer that was running too many programs. When he finished, Berg asked him if he knew where the jig was.

"I don't know where I put it," Alejandro said.

"But you were the last one to use it."

"Look, I just said I don't know," he snapped. "Make a new one. It's not difficult to make one."

"I don't know how to make one," Berg said.

"Just think about it for one second," Alejandro said. "It's not hard. I don't have time to explain it."

Berg walked back up to the shop, hurt and irritated. He thought about their conversations in the forest. Alejandro was such a hypocrite. He preached equanimity and awareness and then he behaved like this, with a total lack of respect. It wasn't Berg's fault that Alejandro had lost the jig. Here he was, listening to Alejandro talk about his kelp problems for twenty minutes and then the guy wouldn't give him one moment of assistance.

Back in the shop, Berg began designing a new jig. It turned out, to his dismay, that Alejandro was right. It was an easy tool to construct and he finished making it in less than an hour. He used the jig to rivet the plank he'd finished and then he took his lunch beneath the buckeye tree.

As he was eating, Alejandro walked past him.

"Hey, did you get that jig figured out?"

"Yes," Berg said.

"Oh, good," Alejandro said. "Well done. Do you need anything from the house?"

"No."

"I'll be up there for a little bit. Feel free to come find me if you need anything."

Berg could tell he was trying to apologize. He'd probably figured out the kelp issue and, liberated from his frustration, become aware of how brusquely he'd spoken to Berg. That didn't make it okay, Berg thought.

After lunch, Berg began to work on his next plank. At a certain point he paused and looked around the shop. His gaze settled on the photo of Alejandro and Uffa from many years ago, the one where both of them were wearing overalls. He was struck, again, by how young Uffa looked in the photo. His hair was long and fine, like some kind of Arthurian knight's. As Berg looked at the photo, he imagined Uffa showing up at Alejandro's doorstep, a lost teenage wastrel who had read some book and thought he knew who Alejandro was. He imagined Alejandro taking Uffa in, those first few days he spent teaching him how to sharpen chisels and how to sail. As he thought about this, something in his heart softened. He realized that he was giving Alejandro no leeway, no room for error. He had made him into an idol, long ago, and if he seemed for a moment imperfect, Berg felt betrayed.

He took the jig from the workbench, pocketed it, and walked over to the farmhouse. Alejandro was in the kitchen, drinking coffee and rolling a cigarette. Berg took the jig out of his pocket and showed it to him.

"This is the new one," he said brightly. Alejandro took the jig in his hands. Berg poured himself a cup of coffee and sat down next to him.

"Excellent job, Berg," he said, holding the jig up to the light. "This is excellent."

CHAPTER 35

SOMETIMES, FOR LUNCH, UFFA wanted to eat a cheeseburger. He was particularly fond of the cheeseburger at the Station House, the diner on Main and Third that was run by Patty McClure. Patty had bought the restaurant thirty years ago, after divorcing her husband in Los Angeles and moving up to Talinas. The menu at the Station House was simple and cheap and there was absolutely no ordering breakfast after 10:30 a.m. because, by then, Patty had heated the grill to lunch temperatures and there was only one grill.

Uffa always ordered a cheeseburger, fries, and a milkshake,

which was served in a beveled glass with whipped cream and a maraschino cherry. Uffa loved maraschino cherries and would ask for extras. Berg normally got a BLT and a cup of soup. They would eat their meals and read the local paper and maybe, if things were slow at the shop, they'd order coffees after lunch and talk to whoever was around. The Station House was usually bustling, full of farmers and high school students and retirees, all them sipping their coffee, the air humming with newsy talk.

After one of these lunches, Uffa and Berg returned to the shop to find Alejandro sitting at the round table, reading a book about bivalves.

"Town?" he said when they walked in.

They nodded.

Berg made his way over to the workbench and began planing a long piece of straight-grain fir. He was shaping a pair of oars for the dory on Celia's boat. After a few minutes of planing, he realized the blade needed sharpening, and he walked to the back of the shop, to the water stones. Right after he dipped the blade in the plastic tub of water, he heard someone calling Alejandro's name from the barn door. He turned around to see Pat the Pilot.

"Pat!" Alejandro said, looking up from his book. "What... what the hell?"

"Hey there, Ale," Pat said. He was wearing a baseball hat and jeans and there was some kind of scab on his forearm. Alejandro stood up and embraced Pat. Berg and Uffa walked over, shook hands with Pat.

"What are you doing here?" Alejandro asked him.

"Just came over to say hi."

"What do you mean?" Alejandro asked.

"We escaped," Pat said.

"You what?"

"We escaped," he repeated. "They sprung us."

"Well," Alejandro said, stuttering, "then... then you shouldn't be here. You should be in hiding somewhere, shouldn't you? I mean, aren't they looking for you?"

"Who?"

"The police."

"Oh yeah, but they're dumb as prairie dogs," he said. "I'm not worried about them."

"What about the other guys?" Uffa asked.

"They're sprung, too," Pat said.

"How did you guys get out?" Berg asked.

"That's a long story," Pat said. "That's a story for another time. I just wanted to come by and say hi to y'all, see my people, you know. I was over in Sacramento yesterday, visiting Lammy. I'm going to be taking off for a while."

"What are your plans?" Alejandro asked.

"I'm going out to Reno for now," he said. "Not sure where I'll be after that. Thinking of heading to Colorado."

"I know a good man out there," Alejandro said. "A rancher and old anthropology friend. Willard Rudin. I'll give you his information. Lives in Trinidad."

"Thanks, that'd be good. I'm hoping to get way out in the backcountry."

"I understand," Alejandro said. He paused for a moment, seeming unsure what else to say. "Well, I'm happy for you, Pat," he continued. "It's a new start, in a way."

"It is. It's a new start for you, too. Lammy said something about a scallop garden."

"3-D sea farm."

"That's right."

Alejandro took out his farming sketches and showed them to Pat. "I'd take you out to see them," he said. "But there's not really anything to see, unless you go underwater. They just look like buoys out there."

After Pat looked at the drawings, he said it was probably time for him to be going. Berg could tell Pat seemed a little unnerved. Alejandro had talked a lot, had explained the drawings in perhaps too much detail. Berg could see this beginning to happen now. Could see Alejandro's mind start to run ahead of itself, to lose perspective. Berg wondered if this was the type of thing that worsened with age. Still, Pat did not seem surprised.

"You take care of yourself, Ale," he said, turning to go. "You hear me?"

"I will," Alejandro said.

Then Pat walked out the door and went into hiding. Berg never saw him again.

CHAPTER 36

BY FEBRUARY THEY HAD launched Celia's boat and Alejandro had settled on a final sea-farming model. It featured columns of scallop lantern nets and mussel socks, which were anchored by oyster cages on the sea floor. The whole thing was tied together with line, from which grew hanks of glistening kelp.

Alejandro seemed pleased with the design, pleased with the whole setup, and the intensity of those few months of experimentation had subsided. He was once again coming in for dinner at 6 p.m., pouring himself a mug of coffee and a mug of wine, and sitting down at the kitchen table, eyes twinkling and beard twitching: the peasant farmer, at peace in his home.

Shortly after the launch, Alejandro and Berg took out the *Darr*. She was a twenty-one-foot-long keel sloop, a stout double-ender with a six-foot beam. Alejandro had planked her with red cedar and pepperwood and he was very proud of her stern, which he considered one of the most difficult things he'd ever built. She was named after Harold Darr, an old cabinetmaker who used to live in Talinas. Harold was blind, stone blind, but Alejandro said he built beautiful cabinets.

"His hands were like living creatures," he said to Berg. "They were always exploring the world around him, feeling, seeing for him."

They tacked their way out of the mouth and headed north toward the ARC radio towers. The towers were the last remnants of one of the first transoceanic radio stations, Alejandro explained. For many years they served as the basis of ship-to-shore communications, broadcasting news bulletins, weather reports, and other information. Their last point-to-point service had been closed in 1973 and was, coincidentally, a connection with Tahiti.

As Alejandro explained these things, Berg sat with his back to the mast, looking out at the hills. It was a clear winter day and the coastal ridge was vivid and green. Thin streams of fresh water trickled over the cliffsides, down the beach, and out into the ocean, where a lone fishing boat idled near the shore, its outriggers spread wide like the wings of an insect.

"Uffa told me he's thinking about heading out to New York for a little while," Berg said.

"I heard that," Alejandro said, nodding once.

"He's doing it because of Demeter, obviously."

"Uffa is never shy about following his heart," Alejandro said. "A few years ago he flew to Italy to meet up with a girl who he'd done acid with, once, at a party on New Year's Eve at the Dance Palace. She was passing through Talinas, traveling up and down the coast. Uffa really fell for her and they had this months-long romantic e-mail correspondence and then he decided to fly all the way to Rome, where she lived, to see her. Spent all his savings. Didn't work out in the end. But I expect Uffa to come and go in that fashion. That is his way and we've reached an understanding about it."

Alejandro eased the main and began to reach toward Bend Rock. They were getting closer to land now and, along the shore, Berg could see surfbirds and black turnstones and wandering tattlers. The ocean swells were green like old copper. Way out, on the curved lip of the horizon, he could see the Slide Islands.

"You ever sail out there?" Berg said, nodding toward the islands.

"Many times," Alejandro said, breathing deeply through his nose.

"Garrett says it gets real rough."

"Yes, you have to make sure to give the islands plenty of sea room. Many years ago, I got caught in a gale out there. It was foolish. I was very young. We had been out on the water for a few days, not keeping very good track of the weather. By nighttime the storm was upon us and we decided to heave to, instead of continuing onward toward the bar, where we would have had trouble. We were in an old Tancook Whaler, which is normally a good heavy weather boat, but for whatever reason, that night, it kept yawing or pitching into the wind. The seas were very heavy, the wind probably sixty knots. The masts were shaking so much I thought they'd snap the stays."

He paused to adjust the mainsheet. In the distance Berg could hear the sound of the water battering the rocks.

"It was my own fault, really," Alejandro continued. "When we'd built this Tancook, I'd recommended increasing the draft, but I hadn't made any adjustments to the rudder. It wasn't a problem in ordinary conditions, but with such high waves and so little headway, we lacked the surface area to force the hull to the wind. Eventually we were able to heave to, after we brought out more sail. And that was when the really big seas started to come. We went down below, is what I remember, and we were sitting down there, watching the sea through the window, when the boat was picked up and pitched end over end. The cabin revolved, gravity reversed, thousands of things fell down to the ceiling, including myself. I remember sitting on the ceiling, looking up at the floorboards and then looking over at the companionway, which was closed but still leaking water, and thinking that I was probably going to die.

"But the boat righted itself," Alejandro continued, "with the help of another wave. We tried to head in after that. We ran warps off the stern and headed for the bar. I was very scared. Very scared and very wet and very cold. It was hours of sailing, and it was completely dark. I traded off with Orhan in one-hour watches. I had been in gales with my father, of course, but I'd never capsized like that. Knowing that the boat had already capsized once, that... that changed me. I hadn't thought it was possible to capsize that thing. We'd sailed it to the Slide Islands scores of times. We thought it was invincible. That's why we rarely even checked the weather before we went out. If we encountered weather, so be it—that just made it more of an adventure."

They were almost at Bend Rock now. On a nearby beach, several sea lions were tanning themselves in the sun.

"That reminds me of a line from Szerbiak's book," Berg said.

Alejandro stiffened, seemed to drift somewhere far away, out of his body.

"Much more courage is required of the once defeated," Berg said.

Alejandro said nothing for a moment, and then he nodded.

"That's quite true," he said.

CHAPTER 37

LATER THAT MONTH, ALEJANDRO began teaching a Saturday boatbuilding class. Berg wasn't sure how successful it would be, but within days it had filled up, and there was even a waitlist. Berg didn't know any of the people who signed up, except for Simon and Garrett. He suspected that they had joined the class primarily to learn more about Pat's escape, which Berg had told them about, but they never admitted this openly. As a bonus to the students of the Saturday class, Alejandro was going to offer a celestial navigation course for free. He invited Berg and Uffa to attend the class, too. It would take place over the next three Sundays.

During the first celestial navigation class, they all sat at the round table in the shop. Alejandro explained that the first navigators learned long ago that you could determine latitude from the position of the sun at noon. But because they could not determine longitude, they had to "run down the latitude," which meant finding the latitude of their destination, and sailing east or west until they hit it. This was obviously a very inefficient way to travel, and eventually methods for determining longitude were developed.

The method he would teach them was known as the intercept method, and it had been developed by a nineteenth-century Frenchman named Marcq de Saint Hilaire, who had, apparently, died of an infection in Algiers after a distinguished career in the Navy. Alejandro showed them the nautical almanac they would be using, as well as his old copy of *Sight Reduction Tables*.

"You know, now they just offer almanacs online for free," Alejandro said. "I can't tell if there's a catch. Like, am I going to get hacked or something?"

"You're not going to get hacked," Uffa said.

"Well, in any case, it's free, which is good, because these almanacs can be expensive. Like fifty dollars or something."

"Shit," Garrett said.

"Yes, exactly. So, in any case, I learned this intercept method from my father in Tahiti. At the time I had no idea what I was doing. No conceptual understanding of the thing whatsoever. I just did it by rote. I was a C-minus student in math, at the best of times, but I was still able to do this, because, as you'll see, once you get it down, it's not too difficult. Taking the sight with the sextant can be harder. Some people have a natural talent for it. I don't know how."

First, he explained, they would be learning the theoretical elements of navigation, and then, for the second class, they would go to Jensen Beach and take sights with the sextant.

"Now, the advantage of taking a sight from land, from Jensen Beach, is that you can figure out whether or not you're on Jensen Beach. And if you're not on Jensen Beach then you have a problem. You are either there or you're not there. At sea you don't have this advantage."

Alejandro drew a globe on the board and then explained how the ancients had divided up the globe into degrees and minutes.

"These are not time minutes," Alejandro clarified.

"What's a not-time minute?" Simon asked.

"Let the man speak, Simon," Garrett said.

"We're talking about minutiae. It's just an arbitrary measurement. It's based on the Babylonian system. Now, in terms of longitude, they decided to divide a day into twenty-four. Again, it's these very ancient notions of time, and they divided a day into twenty-four. So if we were to divide three hundred sixty by twenty-four, what would we get?"

"Forty," said Garrett.

"No, it would be fifteen. So we would get fifteen degrees per hour. Okay, so now I'm going to draw a secondary sphere, which is the celestial sphere, and it's actually infinite, but we don't see it as infinite, we see it as a sphere."

Alejandro lectured for two hours and then had them practice the necessary calculations using a sight he'd taken earlier in the day, at noon, at Jensen Beach. When they finished the calculations, he showed them how to plot their answer on a nautical chart. It was almost perfect. Next week, he explained, they'd head out to the beach and learn how to take a sight.

After class Alejandro went to check on the barn and Berg, Uffa, Garrett, and Simon went over to the Western. Garrett lingered outside to smoke a Black & Mild but the rest of the group went in and ordered drinks. At the bar Berg recognized Ben,

Mimi's Ben, the man who'd helped him after the chicken attack. He went over to say hi. Uffa and Simon headed to the other end of the bar to order drinks. Berg had not seen Ben since he came over and counseled him on Lansing's injury, and it took Ben a second to remember him.

"Oh, Berg, that's right," he said. "Let me buy you a beer. This is my friend Billy."

"Who?"

"Billy," the man said, leaning over Ben and shaking Berg's hand. "You're Ben's friend? I'll buy you a beer."

"Since when are you buying everyone beers?" Ben said. "You're poor as shit."

"Shut up," Billy said, and then he turned to Berg. "Do I look poor to you?" he asked.

"I don't know," Berg said. "Not really."

"Man, you're poor as shit," Ben said. Billy ordered them three beers and Ben put a coaster on top of his, headed over to the bathroom.

"So what do you do?" Billy asked Berg. He almost said he worked at Fernwood but caught himself.

"I'm an apprentice with Alejandro."

"Oh that nutjob," Billy said. "Always trying to rip people off with those dumb-ass soaps."

Then Garrett walked into the room. Billy stood up immediately and stared directly at him.

"This motherfucker," he muttered under his breath. Garrett didn't notice him at first and walked over to Uffa and Simon.

"Hey y'all," Billy yelled to the bar. "A bitch-ass narc just walked in. No one serve the bitch-ass narc." Garrett turned around and looked at Billy.

"Man, I'm over that shit," Garrett said.

"They took away my license," Billy said, walking over to Garrett.

"Well that's your fault, dude," Garrett said. "Shouldn't be chartering twenty people with a six-pack license." Garrett turned toward the bartender. "Can I get a beer?" he said. She poured him a glass, handed it to him, and right after Garrett set down four dollars on the bar Billy knocked the glass out of his hand.

"Billy, you have fucked with the wrong dude," Garrett said, looking up, and Billy punched him in the face. Garrett withstood the blow surprisingly well, considering how unprepared he'd been. He stumbled backward a few steps but maintained his footing. By now Uffa and Berg had positioned themselves between the two men.

"You wahoos take this outside," an old man called from the corner of the bar.

"Bo, I've seen you get in like ten fights in this bar," Garrett said. Bo shook his head and then dipped his nose into his pint glass, like a hummingbird nipping at a feeder of sugar water.

"Let's go outside, man," Billy said. "Or are you too afraid to ditch your two bodyguards here?"

"I'm not afraid of shit," Garrett said.

"Then let's go outside. I'll knock your bitch ass out," Billy said. Then he looked at Berg. "Dude, you need to step off and let me handle this."

"I don't even know you," Berg said.

"Fucking little bitch," Billy spat.

"What?" Berg said, stepping toward Billy. And that was all he remembered from the interaction. He woke up on the floor, with Uffa whispering in his ear. Everything around him seemed to be moving slowly and his ears hummed like a warm engine. He kept trying to say something but he wasn't sure what he needed to say. He felt detached, like an astronaut cut from the ship, floating and waiting to die.

"Can you sit up?" Uffa said. "Do you want to sit up?"

CHAPTER 38

HE WAS IN ALEJANDRO'S bed, still wearing his hospital bracelet. "He hit me in the exact same spot. Right under my left eye."

"You can't change what happened now," Alejandro said.

Berg said nothing.

"Right?"

"Right."

Alejandro took a book from the bookshelf.

"The exact same spot," Berg muttered, incredulous.

CHAPTER 39

"JUST CLOSE YOUR EYES now," Alejandro told him. He had a book in hand now. "Just lean back and relax."

CHAPTER 40

"THIS STORY IS BY John Szerbiak," Alejandro said. And then he began to read.

CHAPTER 41

IT WAS SUCH A strange line, Berg thought. He felt addled, confused. Maybe he'd heard it wrong. He was still reeling from the
concussion. Is that how the story begins? he thought. This can't
be how the story begins. But he had little time to wonder. The
story kept going.

CHAPTER 42

THAT SPRING THE QUAIL congregated in the hills in urban con-
centrations. They marched back and forth through the forest,
clucking and fussing like harried commuters. Everyone in town
commented on their abundance, and speculated as to its causes.
All of the rain from that winter, or perhaps a decrease in the
number of local bobcats, who were among the main quail pred-
ators. Woody had a different theory.

"My guess is that the lizard aliens planted them," he told
Berg, a sober look on his face. "They're priming the habitat so
that it can support them when they invade. They like to dine on
wild fowl. That is widely known."

Apart from the quail situation, it was a normal spring. There were thick oak trees and alfalfa butterflies and yellow-breasted meadowlarks. There was morning fog and afternoon sun and cool nights. Ranch hands roamed the fields mending fences and children snorkeled in Sausal Creek, chasing minnows they'd never catch.

Alejandro was at work on his latest canoe, out on the beach, and Uffa was readying the bus for a drive to New York to see Demeter. He was planning to bring a few musicians with him on the trip and play shows across the country. In the shop, he would daydream about the different things they could do on the tour: play a show in an RV campground in Reno, give away pancakes every morning, record live sessions of the musicians in scenic mountain landscapes. But the organization involved seemed to stress him out, too. He had trouble prioritizing the work that needed to be done most urgently. One day, Berg walked onto the bus and found him looking down at a list, chewing on a pencil.

"Too much to do these days," he said. "Too much to do. Gotta get new tires on the bus, plan this show in Denver, apply for residencies, write a letter to the editor, read these four books. What else? Go surfing, feed the cat, talk to ten different insurance companies... There's a lot of moving pieces right now."

Change was afoot in the barn, too. Rebecca had purchased new seeds, fifty chicks, and several sheep, and one of the geese had given birth to goslings. Alejandro and Rebecca had no room for these goslings, like last time, and they intended to sell them off, along with the goose and gander. Tess was devastated by this and she wrote her grandmother a very dramatic letter about the situation.

"Please save them," it said. "This is too important and we are *all* counting on you."

One Saturday morning, days before the goslings were to be sold, Alejandro and Tess let them out of their pen and brought them down to the pond. Berg was up early and decided to accompany them. He liked walking the geese down to the pond, cup of coffee in hand, and watching them eat bugs and bark and grass and all of the strange things that geese eat.

"There has to be a place we can put them," Tess said.

"Where?" Alejandro asked.

"In the coop with the chickens?"

"The gander would kill the chickens," Alejandro said.

"It would not," Tess said.

"It would," Alejandro insisted. "I've seen it happen."

Tess looked horrified. The gander was floating in the pond. Tess stared at him.

"What if we just kept the goslings but sold the gander?" Tess said.

"I told you, Tess, we have to keep the gander, too. They'd need protection," Alejandro said.

"From who?"

"Any number of things. But coyotes mostly."

"What about that shack over in the meadow?" Berg said.

"It has no roof," Alejandro replied, without looking at him.

The shack had been there when Alejandro bought the property and he hadn't touched it. It was a ramshackle thing: inside there were ferns and nettle growing out of the floor and Berg wouldn't be surprised if a few wild animals called it home. The whole thing appeared to be slowly composting back into the earth.

"The shack would be perfect," Tess said. "It's not even that far from the pond."

"It's farther than I want to walk," Alejandro said.

"But I'll do it," Tess said. "I'll be the one who does it. I'll even sign a contract."

"Will you build the roof?" Alejandro asked.

"I'll do that," Berg said.

"You sure?" Alejandro said, turning to him.

"Yeah," Berg said. "I'll take care of it."

"How lucky for you, Tess," Alejandro said.

And so, in the early days of spring, Berg found himself building a roof for several geese. He used pine for the rafters and gables and half-inch plywood for the roof decking. While he worked, Tess sat nearby, in a patch of nasturtium. She told him about her trips to Horse Island and how Ms. Gans, the teacher she would have for third grade next year, had a mouthful of fake teeth that she removed every night before bed, according to kids in the grade above her. She also liked to talk about stars and outer space.

"I'm a little bit of an expert on the solar system," she confessed to Berg one day.

In accordance with her nature, she grilled him with questions. Sometimes Berg told her that he couldn't answer. The problem was that, once you answered the first question, it usually set off a chain reaction of increasingly urgent follow-up questions, which all had to be dealt with. But other times he wandered into the murk with her.

"Why don't you stay in the guest room anymore?" she said.

"I was recovering," Berg said. "I was injured and I needed to be in a quiet place. But now I'm back in the shop."

"Did you always know you were going to work in a boat-building shop?" she said.

"No," Berg said. "I only started building boats when I met your grandfather."

"He taught you?"

"Yeah, of course."

"I thought you already knew it all," Tess said.

"No, I learned everything from him," Berg said.

They were silent for a moment, and then she said, "Did you go to college?"

"Yes, I did."

"But you never built any boats in college?"

"No, they don't really build boats in college."

"Why not?"

"I don't know. They should."

"Are you going to be a boatbuilder forever?"

"It's what I'm doing for now," Berg said.

"But you don't know whether you'll do it forever?"

"No," Berg said. "Do you know what you're doing forever?"

"No, but I'm only eight."

"Well I'm only twenty-eight."

"Twenty-eight is old."

"It's not that old."

"I don't know," Tess said, picking a nasturtium flower and inspecting it. "I hope I have things figured out by then."

ACKNOWLEDGMENTS

I owe a huge debt of gratitude to Bob Darr, my friend and boat-building teacher, whose generous vision and exceptional artistry inspired this book. I am also deeply grateful to Dave Eggers, who understood what I was trying to do and showed me how to do it better. His support and guidance were crucial. Thanks also to my family: Jesse, David, Rich, and Ellen. To everyone at McSweeney's: Sunra Thompson, Kristina Kearns, and Claire Boyle. To the Urmys, who gave me a place to begin writing. And to Mikayla, for reasons that are, of course, too numerous to list here.

ABOUT THE AUTHOR

Daniel Gumbiner was born and raised in Northern California. He graduated from UC Berkeley in 2011 and now lives in Southern Nevada. This is his first novel.